Spring '98
Supported by AT&T
at the Royal Court

AT&T

shared **experience** THEATRE

ROYAL COURT THEATRE

The Royal Court Theatre presents the Shared Experience Theatre production of

I Am Yours

by Judith Thompson

First performance at the Royal Court Theatre Upstairs, West Street, WC2 on 20 February 1998

I Am Yours was first produced by Tarragon Theatre, Toronto November 1987

Sponsored by Barclays New Stages—Staging the New

BARCLAYS NEW STAGES
STAGING THE NEW

The Royal Court Theatre is financially assisted by the Royal Borough of Kensington and Chelsea. Recipient of a grant from the Theatre Restoration Fund & from the Foundation for Sport & the Arts. The Royal Court's Play Development Programme is funded by the A.S.K. Theater Projects. Supported by the National Lottery through the Arts Council of England. Royal Court Registered Charity number 231242.

FUNDED BY
LONDON BOROUGHS GRANTS COMMITTEE

firstcall
TICKETS · 24 HOURS
0171 420 0100

Funded by
THE ARTS COUNCIL OF ENGLAND

Barclays New Stages – Staging the New continues a six-year partnership with the Royal Court, developed through the ground-breaking **Barclays New Stages** awards and festivals.

This new initiative promotes the exploration of innovation in form and staging, with four new productions and a stage design conference:

- **THE CHAIRS** by Eugène Ionesco, translated by Martin Crimp
  19 November - 31 January 1998

- **NEVER LAND** by Phyllis Nagy
  8 January - 7 February 1998

- **I AM YOURS** by Judith Thompson
  20 February - 21 March 1998

- **GAS STATION ANGEL** by Ed Thomas
  4 - 20 June 1998

The conference will focus on modern theatre design and the needs of theatres in the new millennium.

Barclays New Stages – Staging the New is part of Barclays' broad sponsorship of British theatre, touring high-quality productions through **Barclays Stage Partners** and celebrating excellence through the **Barclays Theatre Awards**. Theatre sponsorship is an integral part of Barclays' overall community investment programme, which encompasses the arts, education and the environment as well as wide-ranging support for the voluntary sector.

I Am Yours

by Judith Thompson

Cast

Pegs	Lynda Baron
Toilane	Ian Dunn
Mack	Daniel Flynn
Mercy	Kerry Fox
Raymond	Garrick Hagon
Dee	Geraldine Somerville

Director	Nancy Meckler
Designer	Gideon Davey
Lighting Designer	Tanya Burns
Composer	Ross Brown
Sound	Simon King
Production Manager	Paul Handley
Company Stage Manager	Maris Sharp
Stage Managers	James Byron
	Suzanne Walsingham
Dialect Coach	Jeanette Nelson
Costume Supervisor	Yvonne Milnes

The Royal Court and Shared Experience Theatre would also like to thank the following with this production: Wardrobe care by Persil and Comfort courtesy of Lever Brothers Ltd, refrigerators by Electrolux and Philips Major Appliances Ltd; kettles for rehearsals by Morphy Richards; video for casting purposes by Hitachi; backstage coffee machine by West 9; furniture by Knoll International; freezer for backstage use supplied by Zanussi Ltd 'Now that's a good idea.' Hair styling by Carole at Moreno, 2 Holbein Place, Sloane Square 0171- 730-0211; Closed circuit TV cameras and monitors by Mitsubishi UK Ltd. Natural spring water from Aqua Cool, 12 Waterside Way, London SW17 0XH, tel. 0181-947 5666. Overhead projector from W.H. Smith; Sanyo U.K for the backstage microwave.

Judith Thompson (writer)

Theatre includes: I Am Yours (Toronto, Montreal); Yellow Canaries, The Leaves of Forever (Young People's Theatre); Sled (Toronto); Lion in the Streets (Hampstead, London; Edmonton, Toronto, Vancouver, Montreal); White Biting Dog (Toronto, Chicago, Vancouver, Ontario); The Crackwalker (Gate, London; Toronto, Saskatoon, Halifax, Evanston, Vancouver, Toronto. Toronto Workshop Production: Walga Wagga, Australia; Montreal, New York, Ontario).

Film and television includes: Talk Dirty to Me, Les Biches, Upstairs in the Crazy House, Teenage Girls Save the Earth, Zero to the Bone, The Elizabeth Smart Project, Angela Wensley - Story of a Transexual (co-writer), Life With Billy (co-writer), Don't Talk, I Am Yours, The Perfect Pie, The Risk of it, Adderly (one episode), Bad Touches, Street Legal - Out of It, Airwaves (four episodes).

As a Director, for theatre: Hedda Gabler (Shaw Festival); Lion in the Streets (Tarragon Theatre & du Maurier Festival, Toronto); The Crackwalker (Vancouver, New York); The Quickening, A Kissing Way (Toronto). For Television: The Quickening, A Kissing Way, A Bit Light, White Sand, A Sense of Home, 8 Minutes. For Radio: Tornado.

Publications include: The Other Side of Dark, White Biting Dog, Airbourne: Radio Plays by Women - White Sand.

Awards include: Two Governor General Awards for theatre; two Chalmers Awards for Best Plays and a Toronto Arts Award for contributions to the Arts.

Lynda Baron

Theatre includes: Maddie (Lyric); Home Truths (Haddon Productions, tour); Pickwick (Apollo, Oxford); Funny Money (Playhouse); I'm No Angel (Nuffield, Southampton); Gypsy (Everyman, Cheltenham); Watermusic (Cockpit, Soho Theatre Company); Lettice and Lovage (Middle East tour); An Inspector Calls (Chichester Festival, & tour); Notre Dame (Old Fire Station, Oxford); Letters From Detroit (Hen and Chickens Theatre); Steel Magnolias (Michael Rose Ltd, tour); Follies (Shaftesbury); Stepping Out (Duke of York's); Little Me (Prince of Wales); Rattle Of A Simple Man (Wimbledon, & tour); Abigails Party (David Kirk Productions, tour); Not Now Darling (Churchill); After Maigritte, The Real Inspector Hound (Shaw); One Over the Eight, Bed Full of Foreigners (Duke of York's); Living For Pleasure (The Garrick).

Television includes: Coronation Street, Paul Merton in...Visiting Day, Two Minutes - New Voices, Insiders, Come Outside, Alas Smith and Jones, The Upper Hand, KYTV, Last of the Summer Wine, Grundy, Open All Hours, Roof Over My Head, Oh No It's Selwyn Froggit, Minder, Mr Gurney and The Brighton, Mesmerist.

Film includes: Yentl, Masquerade.

Ross Brown (Music)

Has worked extensively as a musician, sound designer and composer for theatre. He has also collaboratively devised and performed new scores for over 20 silent films for international film festivals in Avignon, Amsterdam, Pordenone, Lapland, Edinburgh, Llubljana, Rome and Cologne. He has also been an occasional member of the *Mike Flowers Pops*, and with *Adrian Johnston's Ensemble*, collaboratively composed scores for The Four Horsemen of the Apocalypse (Glasgow Citizens); Treasure Island (Lancaster Duke's); Hansel and Gretel (Derby Playhouse).

Theatre music includes: A Winter's Tale (Lancaster Duke's); Orlando, Macbeth, Crime and Punishment, George Dandin, Bartleby, A Story of Wall Street (Red Shift Theatre Company).

Theatre sound designs include: Hamlet (Riverside Studios); Reflected Glory (Vaudeville); The Devil and the Deep Blue Sea, Nosferatu, Turn of the Screw (Shadow Syndicate).

Radio includes: The Affair at Gover Station.

Tanya Burns (lighting designer)

For the Royal Court: Cockroach Who? Mules (co-production with Clean Break). Other theatre includes: Fantastic Voyage, Mensch Meier, Artificial Jungle, One Small Step, 42nd Street, Hedda Gabler, East, The Thirst, Thru' the Leaves, Decadence, The Caretaker (Haymarket, Leicester); Ballad of Wolves (Gate); Funny Money (Playhouse); The Killing of Sister George

(Ambassadors); Red, Another Nine Months (Clean Break); September Tide (Comedy, Liverpool and Leatherhead); Hay Fever (Belgrade, Coventry); All For Love (Almeida tour); Solitude of the Cotton Fields (Almeida); Salt Water Moon, Miss Julie (King's Head).

Opera includes: Powder Her Face (Almeida Opera, & Cheltenham Festival); Soundbites (Almeida / ENO Opera Festival).

Dance includes: Head Shot (V-Tol Dance Co, The Place & tour).

Awarded the Arts Foundation Fellowship for Lighting Designers in 1996. Currently a consultant with DHA Design Services.

Gideon Davey (designer)

Gideon trained at Bath Academy of Art and Nottingham Polytechnic. On graduating from Nottingham in 1991 he was a finalist in The Linbury Prize for stage design.

For the Royal Court: Attempts On Her Life.

Other theatre includes: Night Must Fall (Windsor, Theatre Royal); Great Expectations (Salisbury Playhouse); Macbeth (Sheffield Crucible); A Doll's House, Noise, The Impresario From Smyrna, Song At Twilight, Fatzer Material (Gate, nominated Best Design - London Fringe Awards 1993).

Recent theatre includes: Romeo and Juliet (Chester); A View From the Bridge (Greenwich); Early Morning (RNT Studio).

Opera includes: Peter Grimes (Cambridge); Macbeth (City of Birmingham Touring Opera); Faust (Vienna Volks Opera). Gideon also designed the costumes for Channel 4's new film based on Schubert's *Winterreise* screened in December 1997.

Future productions include designs for Strauss' operetta *The Gypsy Baron* for Vienna Volks Opera, and Cavalli's opera *Giasone* for the Spoleto Festival in America both with David Alden.

Ian Dunn

For the Royal Court: Babies (& RNT Studio Workshop), Six Degrees of Separation (& Comedy).Other theatre includes: Chips With Everything, Somewhere (RNT); Our Boys (Donmar Warehouse, Derby Playhouse); A Prayer For Wings (Tour); Hidden Laughter (Vaudeville); Forget-Me-Not-Lane (Greenwich); Invisible Friends, Wolf at the Door, Brighton Beach Memoirs (Scarborough).

Television includes: Stone Scissors Paper, Gulliver's Travels, Shine on Harvey Moon, Casualty, Bliss, Desmonds, Jackanory, Gulf, The Merrihill Millionaires, The Bill, A Touch of Frost, Soldier Soldier, Children of the North, Sweet Capital Lives, The Saturday Night Armstice.

Film includes: American Friends, Bye Bye Baby.

Radio includes: A Year as a Day, Young PC, Missing Mandy.

Daniel Flynn

Theatre includes: The Tempest, Bingo (RSC tour); Translations (Donmar Warehouse); The Madness of George III, An Act of Faith (RNT); A Chorus of Disapproval (Scarborough, RNT); The Westwoods, The Linden Tree (Scarborough); The Winter's Tale, Anna Christie (Young Vic); All In the Wrong, Love's A Luxury, The Secret Life (Orange Tree); Macbeth (Riverside Studios); The Glass Menagerie (Young Vic tour); Hamlet (RNT tour); Twelfth Night (Ludlow Festival); Woman In Mind (Vaudeville); Chips With Everything, Charlie And the Chocolate Factory (Leeds Playhouse).

Television includes: Peak Practice, The Peter Principle, Bugs, The Choir, Soldier Soldier, A Breed of Heroes, The Detectives, Casualty, The Buddha of Suburbia, The Bill.

Film includes: Biggles, Heidi.

Kerry Fox

Theatre includes: The Maids, (Donmar Warehouse); Cosi (Belvoir St Theatre, Sydney); Bloody Poetry (Circa, Wellington); Jism (Bats); Gothic But Staunch (The Depot).

Television includes: The Affair, Saigon Baby, A Village Affair, Mr Wroe's Virgins.

Film includes: Welcome to Sarajevo, The Sound of One Hand Clapping, The Hanging Garden, Country Life, Shallow Grave, The Last Tattoo, Friends, The Last Days of Chez Nous, An Angel At My Table, Taking Liberties.

Garrick Hagon

Theatre includes: Macbeth, The Fifth of July (Bristol Old Vic); All My Sons (Wyndham's); After the Fall (RNT); Love's Labours Lost, Much Ado About Nothing (Stratford Festival, Canada); Hamlet, The Little Foxes (Nuffield, Southampton); The Glass Menagerie, Toys in the Attic (Palace, Watford); Christie in Love, The Cherry Orchard (Stables, Manchester); American Buffalo (Birmingham Rep); Life of the World to Come (Almeida); . Richard II, The Taming of the Shrew, The Tempest Life of the World to Come (Almeida); Terra Nova, Antony and Cleopatra (Thorndike); Journey's End (Basingstoke);The Dream Coast (White Bear); The Daughter-in-Law (Ipswich).

Television includes: Atlantic, Deadly Voyage, Dalziel and Pascoe, Flowers of the Forest, All New Alexi Sayle Show, Fatherland, Frank Stubbs Promotes, Scarlett, Medics, Red Eagle, Under the Hammer, Sweating Bullets, Revolver, The Chief, Love Hurts, The Nightmare Years, Duchess of Duke Street, Thunder Rock, Stookie, The Adventurer, Lily Langtry, Lady of the Camellias, The Bretts, Julius Caesar, Henry V, Rough Justice, A Talent For Murder, Oppenheimer, Reykjavik, London Embassy, A Perfect Spy.

Film includes: The Opium War, Batman, A Bridge Too Far, The Message, War and Rememberance, Star Wars, Cry Freedom, Antony and Cleopatra.

Radio includes: Mourning Becomes Electra, Our Town, All My Sons.

Simon King (sound)

For the Royal Court: The Call, Drinking, Smoking and Tokeing, Cockroach Who?, Where the Devils Dwell, Faith.

Other theatre sound design includes: Maria Friedman (Hilton); Three Ms Behaving (Tricycle); Scenofest (Central St Martin's College of Art & Design); Cinderella (Adventures in Motion Pictures - Piccadilly).

Theatre production sound engineering includes: Wind in the Willows (RNT at The Old Vic and Uk tour); Maria Friedman by Extra Special Arrangement (Whitehall).

Currently Deputy Head of Sound for the Royal Court.

Nancy Meckler (director)

Nancy Meckler became Artistic Director of Shared Experience Theatre in 1987. Previously, she was a founder member of the Freehold Theatre and an Associate Director for Hampstead Theatre and the Leicester Haymarket.

Her work for the Shared Experience Theatre includes the multi-award winning productions of Anna Karenina and Mill on the Floss (co-director Polly Teale); The Bacchae, True West, Heartbreak House, Abingdon Square, The Birthday Party, Sweet Sessions, Trilby and Svengali, The Danube and War and Peace (co-directed with Polly Teale for the Royal National Theatre).

For the Royal Court: Action, The Curse of the Starving Class.

For Hampstead Theatre: Uncle Vanya, Buried Child, Dreyfus, Dusa Stas Fish and Vi, Sufficient Carbohydrate, The Hard Shoulder (the last three transferring to the West End).

For Leicester Haymarket: The Cherry Orchard, Macbeth, Electra, Orestes, A Streetcar Named Desire.

Other theatre includes: Who's Afraid of Virginia Woolf? (RNT); Twelfth Night (Young Vic); My Sister in this House (Monstrous Regiment); Low Level Panic (WPT).

Film includes: Alive and Kicking, Sister My Sister.

Geraldine Somerville

For the Royal Court: The Treatment, Three Birds Alighting On A Field, A Jamaican Airman Forsees His Death.

Other theatre includes: A Doll's House (Birmingham Repertory); Blue Remembered Hills (RNT); Romeo and Juliet, Epsom Downs, Yerma (Bristol Old Vic); Lady Audley's Secret (Lyric, Hammersmith); The Glass Menagerie (Royal Exchange, Manchester); More Than One Antoinette (Young Vic).

Television includes: Heaven on Earth, After Miss Julie, Cracker, The Deep Blue Sea, Romeo and Juliet, Poirot, Casualty, The Black Velvet Gown.

Film includes: Jilting Joe, True Blue, Haunted, Augustine, Bathing Elizabeth.

shared **experience** THEATRE

The Company

Shared Experience Theatre was founded in 1975 and Nancy Meckler is only its second Artistic Director. Touring extensively throughout the UK and abroad, the company has established an international reputation for its distinctive style of performance and committed ensemble playing.

Over the years, the company has consistently dedicated itself to innovation and exploration:

"At the heart of our work is the power and excitement of the performer's physical presence and the unique collaboration between actor and audience - a shared experience. We are committed to creating a theatre that goes beyond our everyday lives, giving form to the hidden world of emotion and imagination. We see the rehearsal process as a genuinely open forum for asking questions and taking risks that redefine the possibilities of performance."

At Home In Soho

In 1987 **Shared Experience Theatre** discovered the Soho Laundry, a Grade II listed building which had been lying neglected for nearly a decade. The company undertook the complete refurbishment of the building, giving the Soho Laundry a new lease of life and creating two magnificent rehearsal studios and offic space. Shared Experience's productions are created at the Laundry and in addition to the film, TV and theatre companies who use the studios, the building offers facilities to a number of local community groups. In having this permanent home in Soho, the company has become part of the local neighbourhood in which it plays and active and recognisable rôle.

Creative Research and Development

The Soho Laundry has become a laboratory for **Shared Experience** where new projects can be explored and developed. Actors workshops are regularly offered to performers, teachers and directors interested in learning about our working methods. Recent projects have involved a collaboration with composer Peter Salem, workshopping on a new music theatre piece and development workshops for many recent productions, including *Jane Eyre*. Future projects include seminars and masterclasses on composing music for the theatre, directors laboratories, and creating a piece of music theatre involving the participation on stage of young people from around the country.

Youth Education and Access

Shared Experience's Youth and Education work is central to the company's policy of creatively exploring the union of physical and text-based performance. The company's productions are accompanied by a comprehensive Education Programme. In addition, the Youth Theatre, supported by Westminster City Council, meet at the Soho Laundry to participate in a wide variety of drama workshops and special projects.

Shared Experience has recently been working with young people in Westminster on projects which developed the themes of *Jane Eyre*. On tour, the company offers various production related workshops, INSET days for teachers, post show discussions, signed performances, audio-described performances and background notes for schools and colleges.

Recent Productions   Artistic Director   Nancy Meckler

1997	*Jane Eyre* director Polly Teale
1996	*The Tempest*
	War and Peace co-director Polly Teale
	(co-production with the Royal National Theatre)
1995	*Desire Under the Elms* director Polly Teale
	Mill on the Floss co director Polly Teale
1994	*The Danube*
	Mill on the Floss co-director Polly Teale
1993	*Anna Karenina*
1992	*Trilby and Svengali*
1991	*Sweet Sessions*
	The Closing Number director Mladen Materic
1990	*The Birthday Party*
1989	*Abingdon Square*
	Heartbreak House
	True West
1988	*The Bacchae*

Awards include:

War and Peace	Helen Edmundson: nominated Best West End Play, Writers' Guild Awards 1996
Desire Under the Elms	nominated Best Visiting Production, Manchester Evening News Awards 1996
Shared Experience	Peter Brook Empty Space Award 1995
Mill on the Floss	Helen Edmundson: Best Adaptation, Time Out Awards 1994; nominated Best Overall Production, Martini / TMA Awards 1994
Nancy Meckler	nominated for a Prudential Arts Award in 1993 for her outstanding contribution to innovation and creativity in British Theatre
Anna Karenina	Best Touring Show Martini/TMA Awards, 1993; Outstanding Theatrical Event, Time Out Awards 1992

Forthcoming Productions

In Autumn 1998 the company will be remounting its critically acclaimed production of Tolstoy's great novel *Anna Karenina*, adapted by Helen Edmundson. The show, which has been invited to the Brooklyn Academy of Music in New York and to the Brisbane Festival in Australia, will also tour the UK with a London run at the Lyric Theatre Hammersmith (September 14th to October 10th 1998). Future plans include a new production in 1999 of Lorca's *The House of Bernada Alba*, directed by Polly Teale.

For shared **experience** THEATRE

Artistic Director
Nancy Meckler

Associate Director
Polly Teale

Youth Theatre Director
Becky Chapman

Associates
David Fielder
Richard Hope
Liz Ranken
Alison Ritchie
Peter Salem

General Manager
Rachel Tackley

Marketing Manager
Darrell Williams
Office Administrator
Jane Claire
Finance Manager
Bryan Lloyd
Marketing and Admin Assistant
David Brown

Founder: Mike Alfreds

Board of Directors: Robert Cogo-Fawcett (Chair), Councillor Alan Bradley, Marty Cruickshank, Mike Hall, Abigail Morris, Ann Orton, Dallas Smith, Richard Wakely

Acknowledgements
We would like to thank the following organisations for their imaginative and enlightened support:

Shain Jaffe (Judith Thompson's agent)
Great North ArtistsManagement INC
350 Dupont Street
Toronto, Ontario
Canada. M5R 1V9

The Canadian High Commision

If you would like to join Shared Experience Theatre's FREE mailing list, or would like further information on Education, Youth Theatre activities or sponsorship please contact Shared Experience Theatre, The Soho Laundry, 9 Dufour's Place, London W1V 1FE Tel: 0171 434 9248.
Registered charity 271414

AT&T

Spring at the Royal Court with AT&T

The Royal Court is very pleased to welcome AT&T to the Theatre for the first time, as the title sponsor of the Spring 1998 programme.

As a global leader in communications, AT&T is working in partnership with arts organisations world-wide to help make the art of communication meaningful, useful and accessible. AT&T's support of the Royal Court's programme is part of their on-going commitment to new and classical theatre in the UK.

The English Stage Company at the Royal Court Theatre

The English Stage Company was formed to bring serious writing back to the stage. The first Artistic Director, George Devine, wanted to create a vital and popular theatre. He encouraged new writing that explored subjects drawn from contemporary life as well as pursuing European plays and forgotten classics. When John Osborne's **Look Back in Anger** was first produced in 1956, it forced British theatre into the modern age. In addition to plays by 'angry young men', the international repertoire included Bertolt Brecht, Eugène Ionesco, Jean-Paul Sartre, Marguerite Duras, Frank Wedekind and Samuel Beckett.

The ambition was to discover new work which was challenging, innovative and of the highest quality, underpinned by a contemporary style of presentation. Early Court writers included Arnold Wesker, John Arden, David Storey, Ann Jellicoe, N F Simpson and Edward Bond. They were followed by David Hare, Howard Brenton, Caryl Churchill, Timberlake Wertenbaker, Robert Holman and Jim Cartwright. Many of their plays are now modern classics.

Many established playwrights had their early plays produced in the Theatre Upstairs including Anne Devlin, Andrea Dunbar, Sarah Daniels, Jim Cartwright, Clare McIntyre, Winsome Pinnock, Martin Crimp and Phyllis Nagy. Since 1994 there has been a major season of plays by writers new to the Royal Court, many of them first plays, produced in association with the *Royal National Theatre Studio* with sponsorship from *The Jerwood Foundation*. The writers include Joe Penhall, Nick Grosso, Judy Upton, Sarah Kane, Michael Wynne, Judith Johnson, James Stock, Simon Block and Mark Ravenhill. In 1996-97 The Jerwood Foundation sponsored the Jerwood New Playwrights season, a series of plays by Jez Butterworth, Martin McDonagh and Ayub Khan-Din (in the Theatre Downstairs), Mark Ravenhill, Tamantha Hammerschlag, Jess Walters, Conor McPherson, Meredith Oakes and Rebecca Prichard (in the Theatre Upstairs).

Theatre Upstairs productions regularly transfer to the Theatre Downstairs, as with Ariel Dorfman's **Death and the Maiden**, Sebastian Barry's **The Steward of Christendom** (a co-production with *Out of Joint*), Martin McDonagh's **The Beauty Queen Of Leenane** (a co-production with Druid Theatre Company) and Ayub Khan-Din's **East is East** (a co-production with Tamasha Theatre Company). Some Theatre Upstairs productions transfer to the West End, such as Kevin Elyot's **My Night With Reg** at the Criterion and Mark Ravenhill's **Shopping and F£££ing** (a co-production with *Out of Joint*) at the Gielgud.

1992-1997 were record-breaking years at the box-office with capacity houses for productions of **Death and the Maiden, Six Degrees of Separation, Oleanna, Hysteria, The Cavalcaders, The Kitchen, The Queen & I, The Libertine, Simpatico, Mojo, The Steward of Christendom, The Beauty Queen of Leenane, East is East** and **The Chairs**.

Death and the Maiden and **Six Degrees of Separation** won the Olivier Award for Best Play in 1992 and 1993 respectively. **Hysteria** won the 1994 Olivier Award for Best Comedy, and also the Writers' Guild Award for Best West End Play. **My Night with Reg** won the 1994 Writers' Guild Award for Best Fringe Play, the Evening Standard Award for Best Comedy, and the 1994 Olivier Award for Best Comedy. Sebastian Barry won the 1995 Writers' Guild Award for Best Fringe Play, the 1995 Critics' Circle Award and the 1997 Christopher Ewart-Biggs Literary Prize for **The Steward of Christendom**, and the 1995 Lloyds Private Banking Playwright of the Year Award. Jez Butterworth won the 1995 George Devine Award for Most Promising Playwright, the 1995 Writers' Guild New Writer of the Year, the Evening Standard Award for Most Promising Playwright and the 1995 Olivier Award for Best Comedy for **Mojo**. Phyllis Nagy won the 1995 Writers' Guild Award for Best Regional Play for **Disappeared**. Michael Wynne won the 1996 Meyer-Whitworth Award for **The Knocky**. Martin McDonagh won the 1996 George Devine Award for Most Promising Playwright, the 1996 Writers' Guild Best Fringe Play Award, and the 1996 Evening Standard Drama Award for Most Promising Playwright for **The Beauty Queen of Leenane**. Marina Carr won the 19th Susan Smith Blackburn Prixze (1996/7) for **Portia Coughlan**. Conor McPherson won the 1997 George Devine Award for Most Promising Playwright and the 1997 Evening Standard Awad for Most Promising Playwright for **The Weir**. Ayub Khan-Din won the 1997 Writers' Guild Award for Best West End Play, the 1997 Writers' Guild New Writer of the Year Award and the 1996 John Whiting Award for **East is East**. Anthony Neilson won the 1997 Writers' Guild Award for Best Fringe Play for **The Censor**. The Royal Court was the overall winner of the 1995 Prudential Award for the Arts for creativity, excellence, innovation and accessibility. The Royal Court Theatre Upstairs won the 1997 Peter Brook Empty Space Award for innovation and excellence in theatre.

Now in its temporary homes, the Duke of York's and Ambassadors Theatres, during the two-year refurbishment of its Sloane Square theatre, the Royal Court continues to present the best in new work. After four decades the company's aims remain consistent with those established by George Devine. The Royal Court is still a major focus in the country for the production of new work. Scores of plays first seen at the Royal Court are now part of the national and international dramatic repertoire.

GRANADA

▼

GRANADA GROUP PLC

Message from The Chairman, Development Committee

Dear Royal Court Supporter,

The Royal Court Theatre has a track record of success;
I am associated with it because it is uniquely placed to take
advantage of the current climate of optimism, energy and
innovation.

Our plans for the transformed theatre in Sloane Square
include the latest stage technology, a café bar and
improved audience facilities enabling us to anticipate the
latest in contemporary drama whilst at the same time the
refurbished building will bear testimony to our past
successes.

I invite you to become part of these exciting plans.

Gerry Robinson
Chairman, Granada Group Plc

DEVELOPMENT COMMITTEE

Gerry Robinson (Chairman)	Malcolm Horsman
Peter Bennett-Jones	John Jay
Julia Brodie	David Liddiment
Timothy Burrill	Hon. David McAlpine
Anthony Burton	Feona McEwan
Jonathan Cameron	Sonia Melchett
Jonathan Caplan QC	Helen Otton
Ronnie Cooke Newhouse	Alan Parker
Chris Corbin	Maria Peacock
Robert Dufton	Carol Rayman
Stephen Gottlieb	Angharad Rees
Jan Harris	Ralph Simon
Susan Hayden	Sue Stapely
Angela Heylin	Charlotte Watcyn Lewis

We Need Your Support

The Royal Court Theatre, Sloane Square, was built in 1888 and is the longest-established theatre in England with the dedicated aim of producing new plays. We were thrilled to be awarded £16.2 million in September 1995 - from the National Lottery through the Arts Council of England - towards the complete renovation and restoration of our 100-year old home. This award has provided us with a unique opportunity to redevelop this beautiful theatre and building work is already underway at the Sloane Square site. However, in order to receive the full Lottery award, the Royal Court must raise almost £6 million itself as partnership funding towards the capital project.

The support of individuals, companies, charitable trusts and foundations is of vital importance to the realisation of the redevelopment of the Royal Court Theatre and we are very grateful to those who have already made a major contribution:

BSkyB Ltd
Double O Charity
Granada Group Plc
News International Plc
Pathé
Peter Jones
Quercus Charitable Trust
The Rayne Foundation
RSA Art for Architecture
Award Scheme
The Trusthouse Charitable
Foundation

The *Stage Hands Appeal* was launched with the aim of raising over £500,000 from audience members and the general public, towards our £6 million target.

So far the appeal has met with great success and we are grateful to our many supporters who have so generously donated to the appeal. However, we still have some way to go to reach our goal and each donation keeps the building work at Sloane Square moving forward: for example, a donation of £20 pays for 40 bricks, a donation of £50 pays for cedar panelling for the auditorium and a donation of £100 pays for two square meters of reclaimed timber flooring.

If you would like to help, please complete the donation form enclosed in this playtext (additional forms are available from the Box Office) and return it to: Development Office, Royal Court Theatre, St. Martin's Lane, London WC2N 4BG.

For more information, please contact the Development Office on 0171-930 4253.

SUPPORTED BY
THE NATIONAL LOTTERY
THROUGH
THE ARTS COUNCIL
OF ENGLAND

Stage Hands Appeal

Royal Court Theatre

How the Royal Court is brought to you

The Royal Court (English Stage Company Ltd) is supported financially by a wide range of private companies and public bodies and earns the remainder of its income from the Box Office and its own trading activities. The company receives its principal funding from the Arts Council of England, which has supported the Court since 1956. The Royal Borough of Kensington & Chelsea gives an annual grant to the Royal Court Young People's Theatre and the London Boroughs Grants Committee contributes to the cost of productions in the Theatre Upstairs. Other parts of the company's activities are made possible by sponsorship and private foundation support. 1993 saw the start of our association with the A.S.K Theater Projects of Los Angeles, which is funding a Playwrights Programme at the Royal Court, and 1997 marks the third Jerwood Foundation Jerwood New Playwrights series, supporting the production of new plays by young writers.

We are grateful to all our supporters for their vital and on-going commitment.

TRUSTS AND FOUNDATIONS
The Baring Foundation
The Campden Charities
John Cass's Foundation
The Chase Charity
The Esmeé Fairbairn
 Charitable Trust
The Robert Gavron
 Charitable Trust
Paul Hamlyn Foundation
The Jerwood Foundation
The John Lyons' Charity
The Mercers' Charitable
 Foundation
The Prince's Trust
Peggy Ramsay Foundation
The Lord Sainsbury Foundation
 for Sport & the Arts
The John Studszinski
 Foundation
The Wates Foundation

SPONSORS
AT&T
Barclays Bank plc
Hugo Boss
The Granada Group plc
Marks & Spencer plc
Mishcon de Reya Solicitors
The New Yorker
Business Members
Channel Four Television
Chubb Insurance Company of
 Europe S.A.
Tomkins plc

PRIVATE SUBSCRIBERS
Patrons
Advanpress
Associated Newspapers Ltd
Bunzl plc
Citigate Communications
Criterion Productions plc
Greg Dyke
Homevale Ltd
Laporte plc
Lazard Brothers & Co. Ltd
Lex Service plc
Barbara Minto
The Mirror Group plc
New Penny Productions Ltd
Noel Gay Artists/Hamilton
 Asper Management
A T Poeton & Son Ltd
Greville Poke
Richard Pulford
Sir George Russell
The Simkins Partnership
Simons Muirhead and Burton
Richard Wilson
Benefactors
Mr & Mrs Gerry Acher
Bill Andrewes
Elaine Attias
Larry & Davina Belling
Angela Bernstein
Jeremy Bond
Katie Bradford
Julia Brodie
Julian Brookstone
Guy Chapman
Yuen-Wei Chew
Carole & Neville Conrad
Conway van Gelder
Coppard Fletcher & Co.
Lisa Crawford Irwin
Curtis Brown Ltd
Robyn Durie
Kim Fletcher & Sarah Sands
Winston Fletcher
Claire & William Frankel
Nicholas A Fraser
Norman Gerard
Henny Gestetner OBE
Jules Goddard
Carolyn Goldbart

Rocky Gottlieb
Stephen Gottlieb
Frank & Judy Grace
Jan Harris
Angela Heylin
Andre Hoffman
Chris Hopson
Juliet Horsman
Trevor Ingman
Institute of Practitioners
 in Advertising
International Creative
 Management
Peter Jones
Thomas & Nancy Kemeny
Sahra Lese
Judy Lever
Lady Lever
Sally Margulies
Mae Modiano
Sir Alan and Lady Moses
The Hon. Mrs A. Montagu
Pat Morton
Paul Oppenheimer
Michael Orr
Sir Eric Parker
Lynne Pemberton
Carol Rayman
Penny Reed
Angharad Rees
B J & Rosemary Reynolds
John Sandoe (Books) Ltd
Scott Tallon Walker
Nicholas Selmes
David & Patricia Smalley
Sue Stapely
Dr Gordon Taylor
A P Thompson
Elizabeth Tyson
Charlotte Watcyn Lewis
A P Watt Ltd
Nick Wilkinson

AMERICAN FRIENDS
Patrons
Miriam Blenstock
Tina Brown
Caroline Graham
Richard & Marcia Grand
Edwin & Lola Jaffe
Ann & Mick Jones
Maurie Perl
Rhonda Sherman
Members
Monica Gerard-Sharp
Linda S. Lese
Yasmine Lever
Gertrude Oothout
Leila Maw Strauss
Enid W. Morse
Mr & Mrs Frederick Rose
Mrs Paul Soros

JERWOOD
NEW PLAYWRIGHTS

The Royal Court is delighted that the relationship with the Jerwood Foundation, which began in 1993, continues in 1997-98 with a third series of Jerwood New Playwrights. The Foundation's commitment to supporting new plays by new playwrights has contributed to some of the Court's most successful productions in recent years, including Sebastian Barry's *The Steward of Christendom*, Mark Ravenhill's *Shopping and F£££ing* and Ayub Khan-Din's *East is East*. This season the Jerwood New Playwrights series continues to support young theatre with six productions including Conor McPherson's *The Weir*, Meredith Oakes' *Faith*, and Rebecca Prichard's *Fair Game*.

The Jerwood Foundation is a private foundation, dedicated to innovative cultural initiatives supporting young talent. In addition to sponsorships such as the Jerwood New Playwrights, the Foundation will shortly be opening the Jerwood Space, a new arts centre in central London offering low-cost rehearsal and production facilities to young talent.

The Beauty Queen of Leenane
by Martin McDonagh (Photograph: Ivan Kyncl)

The Weir by Conor McPherson
(Photograph: Pau Ros)

East is East by Ayub Khan-Din
(Photograph: Robert Day)

Mojo by Jez Butterworth
(Photograph: Ivan Kyncl)

For the Royal Court

DIRECTION
Artistic Director
Stephen Daldry
Artistic Director Designate
Ian Rickson
Assistant to the Artistic Director
Marieke Spencer
Assistant to the Artistic Director Designate
Nicky Jones
Deputy Director
James Macdonald
Associate Directors
Elyse Dodgson
Max Stafford-Clark*
Roxana Silbert*
Stephen Warbeck *(music)*
Trainee Director
Janette Smith **
Casting Director
Lisa Makin
Casting Assistant
Julia Horan
Literary Manager
Graham Whybrow
Literary Assistant
Jean O'Hare
Literary Associate
Stephen Jeffreys*
Resident Dramatist
Martin Crimp+
International Assistant
Aurélie Mérel

PRODUCTION
Production Manager
Edwyn Wilson
Deputy Production Manager
Paul Handley
Head of Lighting
Johanna Town
Senior Electricians
Alison Buchanan
Lizz Poulter
Assistant Electricians
Marion Mahon
Lars Jensen
LX Board Operator
Michelle Green
Head of Stage
Martin Riley
Senior Carpenters
David Skelly
Christopher Shepherd
Terry Bennett
Head of Sound
Paul Arditti
Deputy Sound
Simon King
Sound Assistant
Neil Alexander
Production Assistant
Mark Townsend
Costume Deputies
Neil Gillies
Heather Tomlinson

* =part-time
 # =Arts Council of England/Calouste
Gulbenkian Foundation/Esmeé
Fairbairn Charitable Trust
+ =Arts Council Resident Dramatist
♦ =Chairman, Development Board
**=This theatre has the support of the
Harold Hyam Wingate Foundation under
the Regional Theatre Young Director
Scheme administered by Channel 4.

MANAGEMENT
Executive Director
Vikki Heywood
Assistant to the Executive Director
Diana Pao
Administrator
Alpha Hopkins
Finance Director
Donna Munday
Finance Officer
Rachel Harrison
Re-development Finance Officer
Neville Ayres
Finance & Administration Assistant
Sarah Deacon
REDEVELOPMENT
Project Manager
Tony Hudson
Deputy Project Manager
Simon Harper
Assistant to Project Manager
Monica McCormack
MARKETING & PRESS
Marketing Manager
Jess Cleverly
Press Manager
Anne Mayer *(0171-565 5055)*
Marketing Co-ordinator
Lisa Popham
Publicity Assistant
Peter Collins
Box Office Manager
Neil Grutchfield
Deputy Box Office Manager
Terry Cooke
Box Office Sales Operators
Glen Bowman
Clare Christou*
Valli Dakshinamurthi
Ian Golding
Elisabetta Tomasso*
Azieb Zerai
DEVELOPMENT
Development Director
Caroline Underwood
Head of Development
Joyce Hytner*
Development Manager
Jacqueline Simons
Development Co-ordinator
Susie Songhurst*
Assistant to Development Director
Ruth Gaucheron
Volunteer
Joan Moynihan
FRONT OF HOUSE
Theatre Manager
Gary Stewart
Deputy Theatre Managers
Sarah Harrison
Tim Brunsden
Duty House Manager
Lorraine Selby
Relief Duty House Managers
Jemma Davies*
Marion Doherty*
Bookshop Manager
Del Campbell
Bookshop Supervisor
Gini Woodward*

Maintenance
Greg Piggot*
Lunch Bar Caterer
Andrew Forrest*
Stage Door/Reception
Jemma Davies*
Lorraine Benloss*
Charlotte Frings
Tyrone Lucas*
Andonis Anthony*
Cleaners
(Theatre Upstairs)
Maria Correia*
Mila Hamovic*
Peter Ramswell*
(Theatre Downstairs)
Avery Cleaning Services Ltd.
Firemen
(Theatre Downstairs)
Myriad Security Services
(Theatre Upstairs)
Datem Fire Safety Services

Thanks to all of our bar staff and ushers

YOUNG PEOPLE'S THEATRE
Director
Carl Miller
Youth Theatre Co-ordinator
Ollie Animashawun
Administrator
Aoife Mannix
Outreach Co-ordinator
Stephen Gilroy

English Stage Company
President
Greville Poke
Vice President
Joan Plowright CBE

Council
Chairman
John Mortimer QC, CBE
Vice-Chairman
Anthony Burton

Stuart Burge
Harriet Cruickshank
Stephen Evans
Sonia Melchett
James Midgley
Richard Pulford
Gerry Robinson ♦
Timberlake Wertenbaker
Nicholas Wright
Alan Yentob

Advisory Council
Diana Bliss
Tina Brown
Allan Davis
Elyse Dodgson
Robert Fox
Jocelyn Herbert
Michael Hoffman
Hanif Kureishi
Jane Rayne
Ruth Rogers
James L. Tanner

SABINA
By SNOO WILSON
NOW PLAYING
BUSH THEATRE
The Bush Theatre and The Long Wharf Theatre, New Haven, CT
PRESENT
THE BRITISH PREMÈRE OF
A QUESTION OF MERCY
By David Rabe
April 22nd - May 23rd 1998
BOX OFFICE: 0181 743 3388

Judith Thompson
I Am Yours

faber and faber
LONDON · BOSTON

First published in 1998
by Faber and Faber Limited
3 Queen Square London WC1N 3AU

Typeset by Country Setting, Woodchurch, Kent TN26 3TB
Printed in England by Mackays of Chatham plc, Chatham, Kent

A CIP record for this book
is available from the British Library

ISBN 0-571-19612-8

2 4 6 8 10 9 7 5 3 1

Characters

Tolaine

Pegs

Mercy

Dee

Mack

Raymond

Act One

SCENE ONE

The stage is dark. Toilane walks slowly towards the audience, on a ramp that juts out into the audience. He is his six-year-old self, in a dream he is having as an adult. He is walking up to what he sees as a giant door, the door of his own home.

Toilane Mum. Muum, I'm home! Hey, Mum, I'm home. Where's my mummy? But this is my house. I live here.

    Pause.

I do so. I do so live here. I do so live here.

    Pause.

I do so. My parents are in there. I do so live here, they're in there. I do live here, I do live here. I do live here. I do live here.

    The 'door' slams. The audience should serve as the door. Do not bring in a real one.

SCENE TWO

Mercy, on a bus, on her way to visit Dee, her sister, sitting next to a stranger, is having the same dream, about herself walking up to that door. She startles awake from the slam of the door. Dee, in her apartment, has also been having the same dream, but she can be standing, willing 'the creature' that torments her imagination to stay behind the wall, and not enter her being.

5

Mercy I knew I shouldnta had that garlic chicken.

Dee There is nothing behind the wall. There is nothing behind the wall.

Mercy Did you ever wake up, well not quite wake up, and you can't remember where you are? I mean just now, I thought I was in my old room at home, where I grew up, and then I wake up and I'm on this bus. I mean it's weird, on Highway Number One, in this dirty old bus, sitting next to a stinking, sleeping old Italian man who keeps leaning on me.

SCENE THREE

The same time. An October night, about three a.m. Dee is feeling faint, needs air, and rushes downstairs to the courtyard where Toilane is leaning against the wall. He stares at her.

Toilane . . . Nice night.

Dee turns away. Dee starts to go.

Hey hey do you . . . do you not know who I am?

Dee (*shakes her head*) No . . .

Toilane I'm the new super. You know, like the super-intendent? So I'll be looking out for ya, right? Fixin your leaky taps, got a problem with the toilet, whatever. The name's Cheese. Toilane Cheese. (*He extends his hand.*) and you go by the name Deirdrena I believe, don't ya?

Dee Dee.

Toilane Oh sure, I can call ya Dee, I'm not formal . . .

Dee How do you know my name?

Toilane . . . the lists, the old super give me a list.

Dee Excuse me.

She starts to go.

Toilane Hey. You got the most beautiful feet. I been meaning to tell ya I like the way they're so long . . . must be size ten, eleven, eh?

Dee runs away.

I like the way they're so long.

SCENE FOUR

Mercy is asleep on the bus. The stranger sitting next to her is an Italian labourer. He is sleeping. Mercy has the dream that follows and in her dream he becomes Raymond, an older man who once picked her up hitch-hiking and became her lover. In the blackout before this scene begins, James Brown's 'Prisoner of Love' should play, from the beginning, starting very loud. Raymond is bringing a rather guilty fifteen-year-old Mercy to orgasm by manipulating her vagina. She has an orgasm, and then immediately pretends that nothing at all has happened.

Mercy God. I love that song.

Raymond It's a pleasant one . . . not like that 'headache' music my kids play night and day.

Mercy (*flirting*) What's wrong, doncha like rock and roll?

Raymond It gives me . . . a headache. (*They kiss.*) Your lips taste like cough drops.

Mercy (*holds them up*) Want one?

7

Raymond No thank you, no good for the tummy.

Mercy I'm up to fourteen a day, no kidding, yesterday I had fourteen, in a row.

Raymond In a row.

Mercy In geography, I mean I was bored almost to death. I mean who cares about the Panama Canal, like who cares that ships can barely get through, like who gives a shit? Anyways, I gotta . . .

Raymond Mercia –

Mercy Yo.

Raymond I – I – I – wanted to give you – this.

Mercy A locket.

Raymond I – I – you'll notice the inscription.

Mercy An *inscription;* fuck, this musta cost you a mint – what's it say? 'Ich' – it's German.

Raymond Yes, it's – read it.

Mercy I can't read German.

Raymond Read it, go on. Try.

Mercy Okay. 'Ich' – that's 'ich' right? Ich – bin – dein? What's it mean?

Raymond It means –

Mercy feels in her pocket.

Mercy Shit. I've lost my penny. Shit.

Raymond Penny? What penny?

Mercy My lucky penny, my mother gave it to me this morning. *Shit*, oh my *shit*.

Raymond tries to dig out a penny from his pocket.

Raymond Well, I've got a penny, will this penny –

Mercy What, are you nuts? You think your penny is gonna replace *my* penny? Give me *my* penny, I want *my* goddam . . . Oh, give me one. Any one will do.

The bell rings.

Oh God, there's the bell. Hurry, wouldja hurry?

Raymond Yes, yes, I'm sure I saw a whole lot of pennies just . . .

Mercy For Christ's sake I got a history test first period, Ray come *onnn*.

Raymond Ahah. Here we are, here –

She grabs it.

Why this is miraculous, you can keep your stockings up with a penny?

Mercy (*sobs*) Okay see ya.

Raymond (*grabbing her*) *Wait*.

Mercy I gotta –

Raymond Please, let me . . . write you a note. I can write you a note.

Mercy Raymond.

Raymond Please I – I've brought prophylactics – I thought today –

Mercy Prophylactics. No! No, no, no! You're disgusting. You're a disgusting old man and you make me feel like a greasy slut and I hate you for it, I haaaaate you, I hate you, I hate you, I . . .

Raymond turns back into Italian man. The lights should indicate that Mercy wakes up. Please don't use

9

any hats or anything to show the difference between Raymond and the Italian; posture, etc. and lighting should be sufficient.

Mercy (*turning away from him, mumbling*) Sorry – I thought you were, I was having this dream, I thought you were this guy I knew before –

SCENE FIVE

Mack, Deirdre's husband, after having been asked to leave by Dee about two weeks ago, has decided, in a drunken moment, that he has to see her. Mack stumbles through the courtyard quite drunk.

Toilane Hey, chief, gotta light?

Mack No, sorry man, don't smoke.

Toilane Well throw you a fish.

Mack Hey man, gimme a break I'm just tryin to get home to my . . .

Toilane No, you give me a break, you give me a break and listen okay, just listen for once.

Mack Hey, man, I don't know you, what're you . . .

Toilane I just want to tell someone, okay? I just want to tell someone that I just seen the face of the woman that's gonna have my baby. She don't even know me, man, but she is gonna have my baby cause ever since I first seen her, in a white skirt with long leather shoes, I felt something. *Green* get it? Like something green like *flash* through our guts together and I knew that I will spend my life, like inter-gutted with this lady, I knew man and I know that when we make love and I don't use the word lightly, it's gonna be like major weather, like *major weather*, I think you know what I mean like major violent weather (*very focused on Mack*).

Mack . . . Oh

Toilane And even tho she don't think I'm shit on her shoe now, I'm gonna git her.

Mack Well. You got your work cut out for ya man. Good night.

Toilane I'm gonna get her and I'm gonna hold her till she's nothing but a warm puddle under my feet.

Mack Good. Well, nice talking to you.

Toilane Thanks for the ear, man.

Mack Right.

Toilane You're alright.

SCENE SIX

Deirdre is finger/hand painting wildly. Mack puts his key in the lock and opens the door. She is very startled.

Dee Mack! Oh, you scared me. What – what – what are you doing here? It's three in the morning. You . . . you should have called, you can't . . . just let yourself in like that, Mack. My heart . . .

Mack I'm sorry. I . . . saw your light on. Been having a beer over at Maydays . . . I wanted to say . . . hello.

Dee You can't just let yourself in like that, Mack.

Mack Your light was on, and I wanted, I needed to talk with you, Dee.

Dee I don't . . . want to talk now. Maybe tomorrow.

Okay? It's very late, Mack, and I'm working. I'm working.

Mack Oh. Yeah. (*He sees the painting.*) Right. Well, if you're in the middle of some kind of . . . creative storm . . . I'll just . . .

Dee No, stay. For a minute. Please.

Mack Are you sure?

Dee Yes. Sit. Do you want some tea? Oh, sorry, I don't have any, sorry. Or coffee. Or even juice. Tap water? Would you . . .?

Mack Deirdre, are you going to sleep tonight?

Dee I'm working, Mack.

Mack But how are you going to teach tomorrow after being up all night, Dee? You know you need your –

Dee I haven't slept for three days actually, and the teaching is going beautifully. The kids are doing fantastic work, brilliant, really, I want you to see it.

Mack I'd love to see it. But I still think . . .

Dee Mack. Mack. It's very sweet of you, really, to be concerned, but I just don't feel at all like chit-chatting because I am working. Maybe I will call you and we can have lunch, okay?

Mack Don't ever fucking do that to me . . . (*He points his finger harder and harder at her.*)

Dee Get your finger out of my face.

Mack Don't ever do that to me.

Dee If you don't get your finger out of my face I'll fucking kill you, I'll kill you, you understand?

Mack You want to kill me? You want to kill me? Okay. Okay. Okay. Kill me, come on. Come on, kill me, come onnnnn.

Dee Get out of here.

Mack Nooo! You want to kill me, you kill me, kill me –

He grabs her fist and rams the knuckle into his temple over and over.

– kill me, kill me kill me, kill me kill me kill me . . .

Dee (*starts to cry*) Stop it, stop it, stop it, Maaaaaackie.

Mack (*he stops, walks away, after a pause*) I don't . . . get it. I don't . . . get . . . why our marriage broke up. I lie awake all night, all night sometimes I've got a burning hole, and I think, I think and I think, what did I do, what did I do, you never told me what I did?

Dee Nothing, you didn't do anything.

Mack It's not good enough, Dee, you wreck my life, you have to tell me why. Why do you want us apart?

Dee I fell out of love. That happens. I'm sorry. I just fell out of love.

Mack I don't believe you.

Dee I'm sorry.

Mack I don't believe you because of your eyes. Your eyes have gone dead. You are not yourself, Deirdre. You are not . . .

Dee What are you talking about, Mack?

Mack You have lost yourself, somehow. Something else is . . .

Dee How do you know what myself is, Mack? Maybe

this is my real self and the other one, the nicey-nicey art teacher everyone adored who made banana bread and sent a thank-you note if you said 'hello' to her, maybe that one was the fake.

Mack Something's happened to you and it's something to do with those nightmares you were having –

Dee I don't have nightmares, the nightmares mean nothing, I don't have night . . .

Mack Dee, you'd wake up and scream for five minutes, five minutes. I'd hold you for five minutes while you . . . saw some unbelievable thing. (*pointing to blob*) What's that, eh, eh, what's that? Come on Dee, I know so much about you. Your mother, your mother. Remember the first time I went up to meet your mother; you were going on about how scared you'd been on the highway, how you would never drive on the highway again and your mother in front of all of us, your mother turned to you and said, 'Why? Why do *you* want to live so much?' Remember what you did? Remember what you did?

Dee Don't.

Mack Remember how you shook, you shook in the sleeping bag with me all night you shook with your head in my arms?

Dee No.

Mack *I know you.*

Dee No.

Mack (*holds her*) You need me.

    Long pause.

Dee I don't love you. I don't.

Mack Nothing? Is . . . there's nothing?

Dee Nothing. Nothing. I'm sorry.

Mack Okay. I don't believe you, but I guess . . . if that's what you say, I believe you . . .

Throws her the key.

Mack walks off. After a moment Dee screams.

Dee Maaaaaaaaaaackie! Maaaaaaaaackie! (*She runs after him.*) Come back, you've got to come back, I'm sorry, I'm sorry, I don't know what, it's like a devil possessed me, I didn't mean any of it, I do love you, I've always loved you, I lied, I don't know why, I'm sorry.

Mack Get away from me.

Dee (*hanging on to his ankles*) Pleeeeease.

Mack Get . . . away . . . from . . . me.

Dee Mackie.

Mack (*a cry from the heart*) Get away!

Dee (*crying*) You're the only person I ever loved, don't believe me, don't believe me when I say those things. I was just cutting my own face, really, I love you, I . . . please? . . . please? Mackie, I am asking you with my whole being, please . . . stay?

Mack I want you to promise me.

We can see Toilane watching them.

Dee Yes.

Mack Never, ever, ever . . . again, okay?

Dee Never, ever, ever again.

Mack Once more, and I'm gone, I mean it, forever.

Dee Okay . . . I promise.

Mack Boy . . . boy.

Dee Oh God, I'm sorry, I'm sorry.

Mack I know, I know you are.

Dee smiles. They are facing each other. After quite a silence they go to kiss very tenderly, but just as their lips meet, Dee speaks.

Dee Youuuuu sucker, you believe me? I *hate* you, I still hate you, I just was scared to be alone, don't you get it, I'm using you, I'm using you, you wimp.

She starts to hit him across the face.

You suck, you suck, you suck, you suck, get out, get out, get out.

She pushes him physically.

Get out. Go!

Mack I'm warning you.

Dee I said get out of my life, and I mean it, don't believe the mewling pisshead in the hall. Believe me, I hate you, I hate you, I hate you.

Mack leaves.

No, stay. Please stay, please stay. Go. Get out, get out. Stay. Go.

She puts her head back and wails.

Maaaaaackieeeee, Mackkkkieeeee, Maaackiee.

As Dee wails 'Maaackie' we hear a siren, louder and louder. She collapses onto the floor.

Maackkkiee, what's happening to me? Maaackie, Maackie, Mackie.

The siren stops. Toilane is in his watching position. His mother, Peggy Creese, a large, uneducated woman of great power, walks in. Toilane is a bundle of nerves, after having watched the object of his love go through such a scene. Throughout the scene, Pegs cleans up the messy room.

Pegs You gotta do something about those socks, Toi, all the men in this family have bad feet. Your father's socks coulda killed somebody on a bad day. I'm serious, like someone who was infirm or in their eighties.

Toilane What are you doing here?

Pegs I'm talkin about your socks.

Toilane Maa.

Pegs Shoppin' bozo, whatja think. Don't look like that, I told ya last night, I said I'll come by six or seven-thirty, we'll go for a bite, and then, we'll start our Christmas shopping. . . . Well it's the third Sarrday in October for buggy's sake, if ya don't start now you'll never get it done.

Toilane I don't have no money.

Pegs Well why not?

Toilane I ain't got paid yet.

Pegs Well that's a fine bed a petunias, how're we supposed to go shoppin?

Toilane I don't know.

Pegs Course if you lived home you wouldn't have to worry about money.

Toilane If I lived home I'd be a retard.

Pegs Why do you say that.

Toilane Cause anyone who's twenty-eight and still hasn't moved outa home is a retard.

Pegs You're outa your gourd. Anunciata next door, the Italian, all four of her sons are still at home and they're in their thirties and forties.

Toilane Right, and look at 'em.

Pegs They're fine boys, that Dominic –

Toilane They're retards, mum, the fat one with the small head? I seen him just standing up on the corner, just standing there at night, for hours, the other one, he's got them cataracts, don't even know he's sposda get an operation and the other one's a fag, is that what you want me to be, eh? A fag living with mummy?

Pegs Oh stop.

Toilane You'd just like that wouldn't you?

Pegs What, if you was a queerbaby?

Toilane Yeah, that'd make you happier than a pig in shit.

Pegs I got nothing against queerbabies, they're good for a laugh.

Toilane Or a kick in the teeth.

Pegs You never.

Toilane No.

Pegs Did you?

Toilane Once in a while.

Pegs Oh that's cute, ya kill any? Eh? Eh? I'm askin you Toilane, did you kill any?

Toilane *No!* I don't know, I don't know, he just kept, like we'd kick his head and he'd move again so we'd kick it again and he wouldn't stop moving and I started seein like a monster from the cartoons with all these snake heads and everytime ya kick one off, it grows another one, right? And he kept growin snake heads so I kept kickin them kickin them off and he goes 'I think I'm swallowing blood' in this voice . . . like Gramma or something but he's a *guy*, he's a guy, right, he's not Gramma, he's makin like he's Gramma and he's a *guy*.

Pegs It's the bad fairy.

Toilane What are you talkin about?

Pegs At your christening, Freida Wilkinson, she hated my guts cause she'd been going with your Dad for five years when I come along, she put a curse on you.

Toilane What are you talkin about?

Pegs Just like in the story, the priest pours the water over ya, you wailin your head off, and everybody comes up to give good wishes, eh, well I turn around and there's Freida Wilkinson, starin me eye to eye and she goes 'Peggy Creese, that baby is in for trouble.' I laughed eh, cause I thought she meant your howlin, but later that night I got the shakes just thinkin about it, I was so cold nothing could get me warm not fifteen blankets, nothin. She put a curse on you, and you lived it out.

Toilane What bullshit.

Pegs Did you kill the man?

Toilane Why didn't you have more kids?

Pegs You know damn well why I didn't have more kids, what the heck are you talkin about.

Toilane So ya stop buggin *me*, why didn't you have more kids?

Pegs Because, because, because my sister's child, Charlene, if you remember, weighed in at twenty-two pounds at six years of age, *six years*, and today that woman owns one-quarter of a pancreas, one kidney and no spleen at all. She *hates* my sister for bringin her into this world, she *hates her*. My brother has epilepsy that's got so bad he has to walk around with a hockey helmet on. I was not about to take the chance of givin birth to another family catastrophe and wear that bell around my neck all my life. No way, no way Jose. Now ask me again why I didn't have any more kids.

Toilane Okay, okay, okay, okay.

Pegs Ask me again why I didn't have no more kids.

Toilane Okay why didn't ya?

Pegs Cause you're the only one I want.

    Pause.

You come home, ya'd have all your meals cooked, your shirts washed, ironed, you could come in as late as ya liked.

Toilane Maa.

Pegs I wouldn't wait up for you. Heck, I'm conked out by half past eight.

Toilane Ma.

Pegs It's easier for me this way, hell I'm livin the life of Riley, sleepin in till half past nine, havin frozen pies for dinner and a bag of timbits, nobody to worry about but my own sweet self. But think about it. If you had all that stuff taken care of and ya didn't have to worry

about nothin you'd have time, time to think, to look in
the paper for good jobs, to go back to school, to get
trained. Trained to do something you're good at. Something you *like*.

Toilane Stop buggin me! Just stop buggin me, okay.
That's why I moved out cause ya keep buggin me buggin
me buggin me. (*Hits something.*) Fuck!

Pegs goes to leave, very hurt.

Maa.

Pegs stops with her back to him.

How's your . . . blood . . . pressure . . .

Pegs High to bursting, in fact I think I feel a bloody
nose comin on right now, yup, here it comes. (*lies down,
gets out a kleenex*) See? Oh yah, I go to the doctor after
Thanksgiving, he puts me on the scale, I've gained ten
pounds, he goes, 'Whatja do, eat the whole turkey?'
Now I did not eat a lot of that bird. Just a wing, a bit of
white meat. Just a bit of soup and a sandwich now and
then. I never touch the pies and pastries.

Toilane Nope.

Pegs And he has to go and be so rude.

Toilane Bastard.

Pegs And then, and then, I walk out the door and I see
Ginny Richardson down the street, about a hundred
yards and that makes me feel sorta better, I mean,
I thought we'd have a little chat . . . then she goes and
sees me and she's across the street in two seconds. She
crossed the street to avoid me, get it? She was trying
to avoid me, Toilane. Now why would she go and do
a thing like that?

Toilane Cause ya talk too much.

Pegs How dare you.

Toilane Well it's true, no one else is gonna tell you Mum, ya got the talk trots.

Pegs Don't you be low.

Toilane It's true.

Pegs It is not true. It is in no way true, and if it is, if it is, I don't care. Because I happen to love the sound of my voice. I think it's very nice and I happen to live alone and I happen to need to talk to talk and talk and talk and talk and don't nobody say nothing because I am talking and I am gonna talk and talk till our feet freeze off and our hands get frost bite cause when I am talkin I am swimmin in a *big vat* of English cream – cream – and talk and I want to swim and cream and talk and talk till we all fall over and freeze.

Toilane Jesus. You running a fever? Mum? What are you talkin about everybody freezing?

Pegs Because we'd be standin outside, outside the Dominion, that's where you run into people, that's where they run away.

SCENE EIGHT

Toilane makes his way up to Dee's apartment. She is lying on the floor. He knocks again and again.

Dee Yeah yeah yeah.

She goes to the door.

Yes?

Toilane Uh – superintendent?

Dee Oh. Yes?

Toilane I'd like to talk to you for a minute, if ya don't mind. Please.

Toilane is silent.

Dee Is there a problem with the water?

She leads him into the apartment.

I've noticed when I turn it on, it starts out dark brown. Come here, look at this. Have other people . . .

She looks at him. He is looking in an odd direction.

Is something wrong?

Toilane No, no, it's not, no.

Dee Are you okay? Are you feeling okay?`

Toilane I'm – I have to tell you.

Dee What.

Toilane Like, it's just that I like . . . I . . . I've seen you.

Dee Is this some kind of joke?

Toilane I been watchin you, and – I – got this – I don't know.

Dee What do you mean?

Toilane I mean . . . I mean . . . I mean that I would lie down on a bed of white hot coals for you to walk over, right on my back. I would fight four black guys, I'd go to the joint and do sixteen years, I mean, I'd lose an eye, a leg . . . I mean I want like, I want . . . to be . . . your knight . . . like. I'm sweatin. I never said this to nobody before.

Dee A knight?

Toilane A knight, like in the stories except now, modern, now, I'd give ya twenty-four-hour guard if you're

23

nervous of burglars or rapists, I'll, I'll fuckin kill anybody that even . . . even if they just say somethin that
bugs ya, I'll kill em.

Dee You want to do all this . . . for me? Me?

Toilane I want to be your knight – with no armour.

Dee Why?

Toilane Because – somepin . . . you got . . . somepin . . .
like *me*, somepin *you* know, you *know*.

Dee No, no, I don't, I don't –

Toilane Yes, you do, Dee, I seen it, ohhh you do.

Dee *No.*

Toilane Let her go, Dee, come on, come on, *now* . . .

Dee . . . (*whisper*) But I'm sooo scared . . .

Toilane It's okay, I gotcha, it's okay . . .

Dee It's . . . okay?

Toilane It's okay. It's okay. It's okay . . .

> *She turns her head in such a way to indicate that she
> is 'ready' to 'let her go'.*

SCENE NINE

Mercy You do so remember, you do *so*, you say you
don't, you're lying cause I was there, I was there and you
were there: twenty below, twenty below zero running
to catch the school bus, all my books fall in the snow,
I gotta pick them up, so I miss the bus, have to hitch.
Stick my thumb out, this guy pulls over, old English
guy in an old blue car, I get in, his name's Raymond,
Raymond Brisson, he gives me a smoke, we get talking

and like he's really intelligent, he's read *Lord of the Rings*, three times, and like, I'm thinking, this guy could be my *boy-friend*. Like none of the other guys at school would even look at me, but this guy, Raymond, he *sees*, see? He sees what I always knew . . . that there's something . . . like a *star* in me, something, like if they *really* knew me, even the . . . truly *great* would love me . . . cause I got – something . . .

So we park at the school, bell goes off, 'Oh my God, I gotta go,' he looks at me, goes, 'You know, you might be quite pretty if you lost some of that poundage' . . . He said that. He actually . . . believed me to be . . . lovely. Lovely.

Not like you you fucker daddy. I *heard* you, I *saw* you giving her that locket 'for my favourite daughter, *Deirdre*' – that heart with the 'Ich bin dein' engraved. What does that mean, anyway, eh? What the hell does that mean?

So he leans over, his eyes going yellow and he kisses me, put his . . . tongue right in my mouth . . . like an egg cracking open in my belly pouring out all this like . . . honey everywhere, *God* I wanted to kiss him again and again. Shit the bell, 'I really gotta go, but but, I think I'll hitchhike tomorrow' then I see *you guys*, leaning up against the wall, having your smoke before class, and I walk by you, almost past you, don't want to be late, when –

'You dropped something.'

I feel my face turning red; like Christ, what if something dropped from my body or something, but I keep going anyway.

'Hey whoredog, we said you dropped something.'

Oh my *no*, that word, no, my heart's falling through my chest, shit, they saw they *saw* your tongue in my mouth, and my underpants, they know, they know, they're all – *shit*, I can't move, I can't move cause I know

25

I know that they know, that they *know* that I'm a 'Hey whoredog. Ya gonna do for us what ya did for that old man?'

I can't cry, *no* please God don't let me, I shut my eyes, waiting, just waiting for them to go in, I still can't move, I'm just standing there, why can't I move when *owwww*. Something hit me in the eye, what the *oww*. O*www*. Stop it, what . . . what – pennies. They're throwing . . . pennies at me, I don't get it, like what should I do? Nobody – told me – how to act how come *God*, *oww* please, how could anyone have so much pennies, and why are they throwing them at me, what did I *oww* oh no, oh no this is so bad please, Mummy . . . when *poof* I know what to do, I know. So I just bend over, I bend over and I . . . pick up their pennies one by one, all hot and greasy, I pick 'em up – they're still hitting my back, till my fists . . . are stuffed, stuffed and I stand up and I walk right to 'em with my fists out like this (*demonstrates*) right up to 'em and I go, I say, 'Here, here's your pennies back.' Then they're gone, and I'm standing there . . . so when I see you, you know, even though it's twenty years later, it's today, you know? It's now like no time's passed, all now and I still can't look at a penny, I can't, cause it makes me know, you see, it makes me know that I . . . am a sick, disgusting whore for letting a guy's tongue in my mouth and especially, especially for letting that . . . honey pour that . . . feeling . . . that I certainly never . . . ever . . . had . . . again.

The old Italian man kisses her on the eyelids.

Thank you, you . . . even though you no *capiche Inglese*, you *capiche*, eh? My girl-friend Virginia? She told me that you only know a guy loves you if he kisses you on the eyelids. Isn't that stupid? Hey, are you cold?

Man *Freddo, molto freddo.*

Mercy Here, take my sweater.

Bus station. Mercy, just arriving in town, runs into Mack, who is just leaving.

Mercy Maaack. Hi. How'd you know I was coming? How are ya?

Mack Fine, okay. Look, Mercy? I'm sorry, but . . . I'm not here to pick you up.

Mercy Uh oh. Is something wrong between you and Dee?

Mack I'm just going to visit my brother for a couple of days.

Mercy Oh no. Oh gee – that's too bad. I was hoping you'd give me a job at your bookstore.

Mack Sure – maybe – later.

Mercy Oh. It sounds bad.

Mack Well, anyway, here's my bus.

Mercy Mack? Do you think it's for – it's not for good is it?

Mack I don't know Mercy.

Mercy Oh. Well, then can I tell you something? I just . . . you know when we would cut green beans together at the Thanksgiving dinners of Mum's . . . did you feel . . . did you ever feel . . . you know . . .

   Mack smiles.

Why don't you miss the bus. We'll go to the washroom,

I'll give you a (*whispers 'blow job'*).

Mack Mercia, stop. You don't know what you're saying. I am your sister's husband.

Mercy You really love her, don't you.

Mack See you later.

Mercy Oh God, I'm so embarrassed, you must think I'm a slut, you must think I'm a slut.

Mack You didn't mean it.

Mack kisses her eyelids. She takes this to have meaning. It doesn't.

Give my best to your sister.

Mercy Yah. Yah.

Mercy touches her eyelids, rubs them hard.

SCENE ELEVEN

Toilane is sitting in Dee's living room, smoking. Dee comes out of the bedroom.

Toilane Hey, smoke?

Dee is silent.

Hey, what's the matter?

Dee Just . . .

Toilane You look nice with your hair messed up, pretty. Hey . . . hey.

Dee Please.

Toilane What's the matter?

Dee I – I want you to go.

28

Toilane Deedree . . .

Dee Please, just . . .

Toilane Are you feelin shamed? You shouldn't feel shamed, you were –

Dee Please go.

Toilane You're beautiful. You're the most beautifullest woman I . . .

Dee Listen, I know that you're the superintendent here, but . . . other than for those kinds of things, I never want to see you. Do you understand?

Toilane But . . . but . . . what we just been through . . . you . . . you . . . can't do that after what we just been through, how can you?

Dee It was nothing, you understand? *Nothing.*

Toilane It was so Deedree.

Dee No!

Toilane You showin me your . . . your animal.

Dee *No.*

Toilane You shown me.

Dee Please go, please –

Toilane No, I won't go, I won't . . .

Dee Gooooo! Gooo! Gooo! Gooo! Get out of here. Get out of here!

Toilane goes to hug her, she pushes him away, she hits him, he stops her, she falls on the ground and bursts into sobs.

Toilane Hey . . . hey . . . Jeez, you must be Catholic or

somethin, are you Catholic? I used to go out with this
Catholic girl, Linda, she'd cry after, but . . . you, you're
acting crazy.

Dee Listen, you said that you would do anything for me.
I just . . . want . . . you to please –

Toilane What?

Dee Leave, I want –

Toilane I think you don't know what you want. I think
from what I seen in there, that I'm what you wanted
all your life. (*Dee sobs.*) Okay, okay, okay. I won't talk
about it, I won't talk about it and I'll go if you want,
but . . . I'll be there, I'll be right down there waitin for
you when you come to your senses . . . and you know,
when I was in high school I broke off with a girl cause
she reclined on the first date, like lay down, in the car,
but I changed now. I still respect ya. I respect ya.

Knock, knock.

Dee (*to him*) Who's that?

Toilane shrugs.

Who is it?

Mercy *Me!*

Dee Who is me?

Mercy Me, for God's sake, open the door.

Dee I'm coming, I'm coming. (*Opens door.*) . . . Yes?

Mercy Dee, it's me.

Dee I'm sorry, I don't . . .

Mercy You don't *recognize* me?

Dee I'm sorry – were you at Joan's the other night, or –

Mercy *Joan's?* Dee, it's me, your sister, Mercy, Jesus, what's wrong with you?

Dee Merc. Merc. Oh God, God, I'm sorry, I'm sorry. I . . . guess . . . I've just been kind of upset – about –

Mercy Mack.

Dee (*looks at her for a second, wondering how she knows about Mack*) Merc, this is Toilane Creese. Toi, this is Mercia, my sister. I haven't seen her in a year and, and . . .

Toilane Nice to meet you.

Mercy Toilane, I've never heard that name before, is that . . . foreign?

Toilane No, not really, my mum named me after our Chinese landlady's son . . . Toi . . . she was really good friends with our landlady, like we used to go to their Chinese New Year's and that, so, you know . . . it's kinda weird, I know . . .

Mercy I think it's nice.

Pause.

Dee Well, Toi, I'm sure I'll see you around the building . . . Toilane is the superintendent.

Toilane Good at fixin things . . . handy.

Mercy Oh.

Toilane Well, I guess I'd better be goin . . . leave you two long-lost sisters to . . . um . . . talk . . . or whatever. (*to Dee*) I'll maybe see you around?

Dee I'll call you if I need anything fixed.

Toilane goes to kiss Dee, she avoids him. Toilane exits.

Mercy *What* was *that*?

Dee How did you know about Mack?

Mercy Why didn't you recognize me, DeeDee, your own sister?

Dee I said how did you know about Mack? Answer me please.

Mercy No, you tell me why you didn't recognize me?

Dee Because . . . I don't know, you're not supposed to be here, you're supposed to be three thousand miles away . . . what are you doing here?

Mercy I came to visit.

Dee How did you know about Mack?

Mercy I'm your sister, why didn't you recognize your own sister?

Dee What do you want me to do, go down on my knees and bang my head against the floor? I'm sorry, okay? I'm sorry, I'm sorry, I'm sorry.

She falls to her knees.

Mercy (*crying a little*) It just makes me feel you don't want me here.

Dee Oh come on, I'm just shocked. You just show up after a year – I haven't even heard from you in three months.

Mercy You don't. You don't want me here.

Dee Whether or not I want you here is beside the point. I want to know why you have come. Where's Tony? What happened? Did something happen?

Mercy Do you want to know where I saw Mackie?

Dee looks.

The bus station.

Dee His brother.

Mercy Yeah, he said something about that.

Dee How did he seem?

Mercy Sad. (*Dee nods.*) Is it permanent?

Dee So what happened with Tony? Are you . . .

Mercy He came home Wednesday night and said, 'I'm moving in with Gina' . . . She's the slut who works in the store.

Dee You had no . . . inkling?

Mercy No. I mean when I think of it now there were lots of things; the fact that we, we'd go out to a restaurant and go through a whole meal without saying a word.

Dee Why?

Mercy What would we say? If I said 'Hey look at that lady over there she looks so lonely,' he'd say, 'What are you talking about,' so all we'd ever talk about was the food.

He had this thing, you know? Where we could only have sex once a week, every Sunday, between the news and the late movie? And once, I think it was Wednesday or Thursday, after work, I had these white pantyhose on and I was feeling, you know, horny? So he was lying there on the bed watching TV, holding that converter, pushing around the channels, and I, you know, climbed on top of him, and . . . sort of whispered to him that if he felt like fooling around, well he threw me right off him and starts yelling 'It's Thursday, it's Thursday you cow, not Sunday, so don't pressure me, don't pressure

33

me, don't ever pressure me again.' So I start crying, you know, just softly and I guess he felt sorry for me, so he says, 'Listen, if you can get it up, you can have it, but I'm watching *The Brady Bunch*.' So *The Brady Bunch* came on and I . . . rode . . . him, I took off my panty hose and underpants and I rode him, here I am moaning and groaning while he's chuckling away at something on *The Brady Bunch*. Do you . . . mind . . . like . . . if I stay here . . . ? For a while? Dee? What's wrong with you, are you alight? You're shaking like a . . .

Dee I'm *so cold*. My body must be in some kind of shock, *shit*.

Mercy Come here. Put your head on my lap. That's a girl, that's a girl. I was shaking when Tony left too, I swear it's perfectly natural after *ten* years of marriage. Of course you're in shock. Oh boy, it's a good thing I'm here to take care of you kid, you need a nurse.

Dee Merc, Merc, you know that fear I used to have of an animal?

Mercy Behind the wall?

Dee Yeah, well it's like something's happened to me. It's like it got out of the wall. Like a shark banging at the shark cage and sliding out. Out of the wall and inside me. I feel something taking over. I don't . . .

Mercy It's just Mack, really.

Dee No, no, you don't understand. I have these dreams, I have orgasms, I have orgasms in my sleep, I wake up with my nipples hard but the dream, the dream that carried it was so horrible, so horrible that . . .

Mercy How horrible could it be, were you devouring Mummy's brains and spitting out her teeth . . .

Dee I'm afraid. I'm afraid that the dreams will seep into the day. That I'll do things – that I'll . . .

Mercy Is that why you broke up with Mack. Dee? Is it?

Dee I don't know. He's the only person I ever wanted. I don't –

Mercy Well, sounds to me like you did the right thing.

Dee I did?

Mercy Well yes. I mean, a man would bring this thing forth, wouldn't he? Or a baby. Dee, you mustn't have a baby.

Dee Why?

Mercy Who knows what might happen. Who knows what you could do. You could do horrible things. Mum knew that about you – Dee? Knife old ladies in the head. Screw old winos in the park. When people let their animal out they go to the top of tall buildings and shoot forty people.

Dee Oh God.

Mercy I know you Dee, I'm your sister. Mum knew you. I know what you could do. No, you don't want Mackie. I'm here now. I'll take care of you. I know you. Poor baby, you're really still a baby, aren't you?

Dee Sing that song, sing that song you used to sing when I was little and scared of the animal, sing that song.

Mercy
 Weee . . . are . . . walking . . . togetherrr in the nice
  weatherrrr
 Ohhh what a lovely dayyyy . . .
 Weee are walking togetherrrr in the nice weatherrr . . .
 Ohhhh what a lot of fuuuunnn . . .

Dee joins in; after, she falls asleep.

You know when you have wild sex with a guy like that they stick to you like glue. I mean, I know you probably had to do something wild cause of Mackie, but how are you going to get rid of him?

Dee is asleep. Mercy smiles.

We are . . . walking . . . together . . . in the ni-ice . . .
   weather,
Oh what a lovely . . .

SCENE TWELVE

Mack comes out on ramp the same way Toilane did, addressing the audience.

Mack When I was nine I was stung by a thousand bees; one hundred fifty-seven stingers in my nine-year-old body, I was on a respirator for three days. I can still feel it, hear it. My mother, Joy, was a cleaning fanatic, obsessed: every time you opened our front door, you'd hear *vrooooooom*, she vacuumed twice a day, you'd almost pass out from the fumes of the bleach and the Pine Sol. I always slipped on the overwaxed floor. She'd have done three or four loads of laundry before she woke up my sister and me at seven; she washed the kitchen floor with straight bleach every day.

I remember the first, the first bee, I was about nine and I was having a glass of milk after my soccer game, in the kitchen, she was standing over me waiting to clean it, and there was this buzzing. *Bzzzzzz bzzzzzz*, my mother looked around, *bzzzzz*, and then it stung her, on the hand. Her hand swelled up badly, she ran the cold water. *Bzzzzz*, I spotted another, by the fridge, and then another on the ceiling, she was frantic. We opened the pantry and although everything was, like, perfectly stored and packaged there were four or five or six of these bees buzzing around. One of them came after me, it actually chased me. I ran to the third floor, it chased me all through the house and then stung me hard on the lip, it hurt so much. My mother, she stood in the pantry like a cat, watching the walls, trying to figure out where they were coming from. I'm watching TV, suddenly *wham bash*, I run to the pantry and there is my mother, my clean mother smashing in the pantry wall with my baseball bat. Down came the plaster, filling the air with dust, and then the lath, and then she's tearing away the pink insulation, sobbing and choking, and I'm trying to see through all this dust. The buzzing sound was deafening like the bass of an electric guitar turned way way up, and there it was . . . huge, majestic, a shimmering tower of bees, a six-foot honeycomb, dripping, behind our wall, hundreds, no, thousands of bees swarming around it protecting their queen, all for the queen, and they swarmed us, stung us, over and over, the honey poured thick from the hive, into our pantry, into our house, unstoppable over bleached linoleum floor and into the hall, seeped in the carpet . . . And since that time I have thought, I have known that there is some-thing deadly, yes, but I don't know really . . . glorious behind every wall. Deirdre. Her fear of things behind walls? Her eyes?

SCENE THIRTEEN

Dee is on the phone to the pharmacist. We see her canvas, which she has painted with a black line inside a brilliant yellow circle. Only she and the canvas are lit.

Dee Hi, I bought a pregnancy test from you this morning,

37

and I seem to have lost the instructions . . . could you tell me what a black line means? A black line inside a brilliant yellow circle?

Toilane is watching her, from his glass door. He sits and smokes and watches.

SCENE FOURTEEN

Hospital. Dee, having left her pre-surgery bed and wandered down the halls, in her gown, walks towards the audience as we hear the doctors paged. She has felt the life of the foetus inside her and cannot go through with the abortion. She now walks towards the audience: she addresses the audience as if it is the foetus.

P.A. Calling Doctor Samuels, Doctor Samuels to Emerg, Doctor Samuels, calling Doctor Rank, Doctor Rank to the O.R., Doctor Rank, calling Doctor Johnson, Doctor Deborah Johnson to Maternity, Doctor Deborah Johnson, calling Doctor Roch, Doctor Roch please, calling Doctor Domovitch, Doctor Domovitch, calling Doctor French, Doctor French . . .

Dee A feeling like a push; somebody strong, pushing me off the table, it was not a . . . decision, I was pushed and I felt and I feel and I hear . . . a breathing . . . inside me, that is not my own. I do . . . hear it. A raspy kind of sweet breathing a – a – pulling for breath, for air and kind of a sigh of content. I feel the breath on my face the drops of wet breath, hear a sigh, are you there? A voice not mine, a voice like no other; there you are, in the sighing, and I know I think I know whose voice this is; this is yours, this is yours, this is not a mirage, no, not part of the madness, a moment of clear, oh yes, you are clear, I can taste your sweet breath, a flower,

38

not mine, not mine but inside me I can feel on my hand
the press of your hand, fingers, holding my hand, tiny
fingernails, not letting go, the impression, the feel of a
tiny body lying next to mine, breathing, in the bed,
cream sheets. I am asleep; how can I see this? How?
You are showing me, showing me, you are looking at
me with your dark blue eyes, staring at me in the dark
in the night, smelling my milk, breathing fast for my
milk, the shininess of your eyes like the moon on the
water I see: I see it, in my mind, too clearly, just as I can
hear your voice, too too clear, rising, falling, your eyes,
looking at me from across the room, watching me move
across the kitchen, watching me; when I hold you and
you wrap my hair around your tiny hands, pulling, and
your head on my chest rooting for the breast, I can hear,
I can feel the rooting. I am lost, I have heard you, I can
feel you drinking of me, you drink my milk and you
drink and you drink and oh, I am lost.

SCENE FIFTEEN

*Dee, still in her hospital gown, at home with Mercy. On
her canvas is the grotesque painting of a ten-week-old
foetus.*

Dee I could hear it, Mercy, I could see it, see it, sending
these flashes, these flashes of life.

Mercy You're telling me that you were lying on the bed,
all ready to be wheeled into the operating room, the
poor gynaecologist was putting on his scrubs and you
took off? You just left?

Dee You don't understand.

Mercy You're not allowed to do that, Dee.

39

Dee But I saw it. I saw the life that I was about to have *sucked, vacuumed* –

Mercy Oh my God you haven't gone *pro-life* on me.

Dee *It's not okay.* It's not okay to take this life this life is *living*.

Mercy Bullshit, Dee, bullshit, I've been pregnant three times, *three*, and I've never felt a thing, the thing is like an *insect*.

Dee Nooooo.

Mercy You think I'm some kind of *butcher*?

Dee You're asleep, that's all, you don't know what you're doing, this . . . child . . . woke me up.

Mercy Okay, well, what are you going to do then, Pollyanna? What are you going to do? . . . Could you suckle a baby with Toilane's face? Could you, Dee? Deedee? Aren't you afraid of what your *animal* might do? Look at the girl on the news last night who threw her baby into the lake, Dee, what are you going to do?

Dee I don't know.

Mercy Are you going to give it to him, to Toilane?

Dee stares at Mercy.

You have to decide, Dee. You can't just not know. You have to decide.

Mercy shakes her.

Deirdre.

Dee Leave me alone. Leave me alone. Do you hear me? Leave me –

Toilane, who has been listening at the door, opens it.

40

Toilane It's funny, I sorta knew I madja pregnant. I pictured, you know? While we were doin it. I pictured in my mind, this face, lookin at me, this . . . face.

Dee Listening at people's doors is a criminal offence.

Toilane I want to marry you.

Dee It was a one-night stand, Toi.

Toilane Don't be ashamed, please, don't be ashamed. I love you. I want to marry you, I want – our child together, I –

He offers a ring, she kicks it away.

Dee Will you wake up? I'm having this baby and I am giving it away. Get it? Get it?

Toilane You're giving my baby away? You're givin my baby away?

Dee I'm giving your baby away, yes.

There is a long pause. Toilane goes down to the courtyard to cry.

Mercy That was a hideous thing to do.

Dee (*starts changing*) Fuck off.

Mercy That was a disgusting, cruel, horrific . . .

Dee Get off my case, Mercia.

Mercy No, no, this time I will not get off your case.

Dee Oh cut the sabre-toothed tiger routine, really.

Mercy You make me sick you are so smug and beautiful, you have no idea what it is to be me, all the boys looking straight at you, never at me. That time at the dance when you went right up to Stephen Gilroy who you knew was crazy about you and said, 'Oh dance with

41

Mercy, she loves you so much.' And the other time in front of all our friends when you made me pick my nose and eat it; you said I had to, to get in your club, that you'd all done it. And then I did it. And you laughed, you laughed. Do you know how much I hated you? Do you know how much?

Dee Oh come on Mercia.

Mercy If you're a woman and you're born ugly you might as well be born dead. Don't. Don't you laugh.

Dee Mercia, listen to me. You can whine all you like about being fat and ugly but it was your choice. You *chose* to look like that, I chose to look like this. I *chose* it because I needed to *please*. You do not need to please, do you know how lucky you are? Do you know?

Mercy If you are a woman and you are born ugly you might as well be born . . . dead.

Dee Oh really Merc, I think you've been watching too much television.

Mercy Don't put down television. *Don't you fucking put down television*, you snot, television has saved my life. It has literally saved my life, when you're so lonely you could die. I mean shrivel up and die because nobody cares whether you get up or stay in bed or don't eat, when you're so lonely every pore in your skin is screaming to be touched, the television is a saviour. It is a voice, a warm voice. There are funny talk shows with hosts who think exactly like I do. And when the silence in your apartment, the silence is like a big nothing and you're thinking, my God, my God, is this what life is? Years and years and years of this? You turn on the television and you forget about it. Often all I'll think about all day at work is what's on TV that night, especially in the fall, with the new shows, I get really, genuinely excited. I . . . I love television. I love it. It makes me happy so don't put it down.

She exits.

SCENE SIXTEEN

Mack goes through the courtyard. He sees Toilane sobbing against the wall. Mack stops, looks at Toilane.

Mack I hope whatever it is . . . passes.

Mack knocks on Dee's door. The grotesque painting of a three-month foetus is replaced by a beautiful one of a four-month foetus

Dee Hi. Come in. Can I get you some tea?

Mack Sure. Okay.

Dee It looks like quite the storm out there.

Mack Biggest one of the season they say.

Dee Yah?

Mack Yeah.

Dee So, how have you been?

Mack Oh, oh, you know; okay. Look, Dee is this just a visit or –

Dee I wanted to see you. I've missed you so – I feel it all here. (*Puts her hand on her chest.*) It's like this great weight here. Do you ever . . .

Mack *Don't.*

Dee I try not to think about you but then I dream about you every night. Last night you were holding my skull in

43

fragments – like a teacup and you held it together – in your hands – you –

Mack Dee, forget it.

Dee I know I have no right at all after my terrible behaviour but – every footstep on the stair, Mack, your voice . . .

Mack Don't play with me, please don't.

Dee I'm serious, Mack.

Mack Yeah, just like my two-year-old nephew says, 'I want juice,' and then you give it to him and he throws it on the floor.

Dee No. No, not like your two-year-old nephew, I'm serious. Look, what I said before, that night, it was like an illness. An infection or something. Encephalitis. I don't know. Whatever it is, it's gone. It's gone and it'll never happen again. I wanted to call you for a while now, but I was scared, afraid, really. I've been watching out the window every day in case you –

Mack gets up to go.

Mack, I want you to come back.

Mack How can I know if you're serious?

Dee Well for one thing I'm pregnant.

Mack So, what, you want me to hold your hand on the way to the clinic, be there when you come out of the anaesthetic?

Dee I'm keeping this one. I'm already three and a half months. Mack, it – spoke to me – I literally got up off the stretcher and walked out of the *hospital*. Mack – Mack?

Mack You walked out of the hospital?

44

SCENE SEVENTEEN

Pegs sees Toilane sobbing on the ground in the court-yard. She approaches him.

Pegs I don't know if you lost your job or some girl give ya your walking papers, but whatever it is, I don't think you'd want your father to see you take it lying down. Get up Toi. Get up off the ground.

SCENE EIGHTEEN

Mack and Mercy are chopping green peppers, hard on large wooden block. First we hear the chopping sound. Mercy is aroused. We see Mack become aware of this and move away.

Mercy So uh, I hate to be like nosy, but, like are you guys back together? You spend an awful lot of time in the bedroom.

Mack How small do you want these things anyway?

Mercy Oh Mack, stop being such a *guy*, are you together or not?

Mack Yes.

Mercy What happened?

Mack You are a sticky beak.

He puts a vegetable on her nose.

Mercy I just think it's ridiculous.

Mack Awwww.

Mercy Well, she doesn't love you.

Mack Hey, hey, easy.

Mercy Well, she doesn't. I might as well tell you the truth. She's told me.

Mack (*sings*) Here we go a chopping greens, chopping greens, chopping greens . . .

Mercy Are you staying because of the baby?

Mack You shut your mouth and keep chopping.

Mercy But you're happy about the baby?

Mack smiles.

Why her? Why her Mack? What . . . does she have?

Mack Come on, Merc, don't . . .

Mercy I just want to know, after she treats you like absolute *shit* on her *shoe*, what is it you see in her?

Mack She doesn't have your nice big bum, that's for sure.

Mercy Don't patronize me. I want to know what you see in her.

Mack I'm sorry, what can I say?

Mercy (*approaching him*) Do you find me at all attractive?

Mack Yes, of course, you're very attractive.

Mercy Would you . . . kiss me?

Mack Merc . . .

Mercy Please? Nobody's kissed me in so long. My husband never kissed me, not for years, we'd just do it in the dark facing separate directions. Please?

Mack walks towards her, kisses her, a nice, long kiss, she wants more, he backs off, pats her on the back in a friendly way.

46

Oh the weight, the weight of a man, you know? I miss that weight. Hey, you've got lipstick on your face, really.

Dee puts her key in the door, comes in.

Dee I just had the most amazing cab driver. He'd been driving for forty-two years, *forty-two*, he was three years in the marines and then he got his hack licence, he told me, he said, 'I hate this city, I hate the other cabbies, I hate the road and most of all, most of all,' he says, 'I hate the riding public.' Don't you love that, 'the riding public'? – Where're you going?

Mack Shit. I have to be at the store in . . . four minutes ago.

Dee Aren't you eating dinner with us?

Mack Yeah, yeah, yeah, this is just a meeting, I have a meeting, it's one-third my store, I should be there.

Dee (*kisses him*) Okay. See you soon.

Mack Bye Merc.

He leaves.

Dee (*still laughing, putting down bags*) 'The riding public,' I love that.

Mercy *How could you do that?*

Dee What?

Mercy Tell him that it's *his* baby, don't you think he'll be suspicious when the kid doesn't look anything like him?

Dee I told you, I'm giving it away, the Children's Aid has the *perfect* couple.

Mercy Does he know that?

Dee No.

47

Mercy Well, when are you going to tell him, you have to tell him.

Dee When I'm sure I have my roots in him.

Mercy What about your animal or whatever it was. Aren't you *terrified* you might –

Dee Oh that, that was just – I was under a huge amount of pressure at work, it . . .

Mercy Bullshit, it's not gone, it's taken over you. It is you. You're body-snatched. That's why you're behaving so atrociously.

Dee How am I behaving?

Mercy Using Mack, using . . .

Dee Fuck off do you hear me? I don't want to hear another fucking word about Mack. I don't want to hear . . .

Mercy begins to freak out, she rips newspaper in Dee's face and screams.

Mercy I want . . . to be the centre, I want to be the centre of somebody's life. I haven't been the centre since Mum died, she made me the centre, she sat up when I came in, she asked me what I got at the store and how was the bank today and didn't think I was overqualified for my work. She said I looked tired and it was too cold for me out there and nobody does that. *Nobody*.

You know, I'm so . . . stupid, so loathsome that I actually, I had this friend in Vancouver, that was dying of a brain tumour, and I wished on my birthday, I wished that I would get one so that I could have that kind of kindness . . . from people.

Pause.

How can anybody like me, eh? How can you like me?
I mean would you like me if I wasn't your sister? Would
you?

Dee You were very kind to me when I was little. You're
a very . . . kind person.

SCENE NINETEEN

Pegs and Taxi Driver.

Pegs Your children are only loaned to you, that's what
Muriel said; they're only loaned to you for a short
time . . . It comes as quite a shock to us, you know, us
girls who been brought up to think family is our whole
life and ya grow up and ya get married and ya start havin
kids and you are in your prime, man, everybody on the
street smiles, they respect ya, you're the most powerful
thing there is, a mother, with young kids, and the kids
think you're Christmas, they want to sit on your knee,
and help ya bake cookies, Mum this, Mum that, and
you're tired as hell but you're having the time of your *life*,
right? You're important, you're an important member of
society, kids all around you, friend's kids, sister's kids, car
pools, Round Robin – you're havin a ball. And then they
get older, ya go back to work, and it's their friends, their
friends are more important than you, than anything in the
world, ya couldn't drag them out on a picnic for a million
dollars, and it seems they only talk to you if it's to get
money or the car. They whip through their meals in about
ten seconds flat, something took you five hours of buying
and chopping and mixing and cooking, and then they
leave the house. And ya never see em, and ya wonder if
they hate you. You know they're only there because of the
money thing, they'd be gone in a second if there was a
chance. Why is that? Why don't they like you anymore? I

49

tried; you know, I tried like hell to listen to the AC-DC and the Led Zepplin and all that, even said I liked it, I did like that 'Stairway to Heaven' one, I used to get jokes from the magazines, newspapers, you know, a Mum with a sense of humour? That went over like a lead balloon. I'd drive him to his parties, his roller skatin, his hockey and baseball, we'd go the whole drive silent, not a single word. Only word was at the end, 'Pick me up at eight o'clock.' . . . What happened? What happened to the baby who looked up at me with eyes when the doctor first showed him to me, blackberry eyes, the baby I musta walked ten miles a day in our little apartment, back and forth, back and forth, eyes closin, lookin at me, lookin at me. Why is it that look goes away?

Driver Three seventy-five, please, lady.

Pegs I know. I know how much it is.

SCENE TWENTY

Mercy, Mack and Dee are all sitting around having after-dinner drinks.

Mack So, Dad *dies* at the top of the stairs, massive heart attack right on the top stair well, Lucy, our *dog* was at the bottom, she goes berserk, howling like a banshee, wouldn't let a soul near him, they had to shoot her with a stun gun; two days later she has a stroke, you'd go into the house, it's pitch dark and there was my mother passed out on the couch with a bottle of Scotch and this *dog* with a paralysed bark.

Mack renders a dog's paralysed bark.

Dee She's a sweet dog, golden Labrador.

Mercy Uh oh, I can feel my boils starting.

Dee What do you mean?

Mercy Every time I drink red wine I get boils, it's incredible, these huge red things and if I try and squeeze them they just go to twice the size, it's a curse.

Mack Well when you hear what they put in wine these days.

Dee Anti-freeze.

Mack What?

Dee Whatever the scientific word for anti-freeze is, that's what they put in, I think.

Mack So, Mercy, you haven't said a word about your new job. Are you bored to death?

Mercy Apparel can be really interesting you know. I used to work lingerie, and I got so I could tell a girl's size as soon as she walked through the door, winter coat and everything, she'd come in right? And she'd say, 'I'd like a 36B please,' and I'd go, 'I'm sorry but you're not gonna need anything bigger than an "A",' and she'd get all huffy with me but then she'd try it on and I'd be right. She'd go, 'How'd you know?' and I'd go, 'I don't know, I just know.' I just knew.

Mack But . . . how?

Mercy Ohh it's a talent, I guess, a creative talent.

Mack Come on, you're trying to tell me you could guess somebody's bra size under a winter coat?

Mercy Yes Mack, why, do you think I'm lying? Do you think I would lie about it?

Dee He's not suggesting you're lying Merc, we're just wondering how you could determine a woman's bra size if she's wearing a coat.

Mercy . . . From her face to tell you the truth. Girls
of different bra sizes wear different faces, like, if you're
a 28, right, you've been that all your life, so you have
a certain . . . you're all looking at me thinking I'm
incredibly stupid.

Mack I know what you mean. I . . . have the same talent
with suit size.

Mercy . . . Suitcase.

Dee What?

Mercy The word suitcase means suit . . . case, like case
for suits, did you ever think of that? I mean it's amazing,
I just never . . . thought of it . . .

Knock, knock, knock at the door; repeats.

Mack (*joking*) Go away. Go away.

Mercy I'll get it.

Mack No, I'll get it.

Mercy No, I'll get it.

Mack No, I'll get it.

Mercy No, I'll get it.

Mack Okay, you get it.

*Mercy gets it. It is Pegs and Toilane. Pegs pushes
Mercy out of the way.*

Pegs (*now addressing the room*) The heck with this. The
heck with this. (*Snaps her fingers.*) Toi. Come on, we're
gonna have a talk with these people.

Dee Pardon me, I don't believe . . .

Pegs Asked or not, we're comin honey and you're sitting

down and you're gonna listen up. Sit down.

Dee No. I don't have to sit down, what are you . . .

Pegs You know damn well why I'm here, now sit down.

Mack Sit down Dee, the lady has something to say. Spice things up a little.

Dee Mack, I . . .

Mack Come on. We'll all sit down.

Dee If you don't leave I'm calling the police.

Mack Oh my God there's no need to bring the police into this my dear, let's listen to what the woman has to say.

Dee Well, I'm leaving then, you can all stay here.

Mack Dee, come on, relax.

Pegs Enough of this stupidity. You are gonna give my grandchild away over my *dead body*.

Terrible pause.

You hear me?

Dee I'm sorry, I really don't know what you're talking about.

Pegs You know damn well what I'm talking about slut, and you're not gettin away with it. I got the best lawyer in this city workin on the case and we are gonna win hands down. And not only are we gonna get our baby, but you are gonna pay us for damages through the *teeth*, understand?

Dee I'm sorry, I really think you have the wrong apartment.

Mack What is this?

53

Pegs You the husband are ya? How's it feel to be married to a two-timin' slut who gives babies away?

Mack Look, I'm sure this has all arisen from a mis-understanding, surely we can . . .

Pegs There's no misunderstandin here. Your wife had sexshul relations with my son . . . on this floor . . . and made him do funny things. After I spent twenty-three years teaching him to respect a woman. And then she told him herself that she was pregnant with his kid, and that she was gonna give it away. Cause she didn't want her baby with people like us. Am I right?

Dee Look, Mrs . . .

Pegs Creese, Margaret Creese.

Dee Mrs Creese, your son, came up one day to borrow some milk, or that was the excuse he made, and then he proceeded to assault me; he ripped my blouse and held a knife to my throat and I don't know what else he would have done had my sister not come in.

Mack What is going on? Did this guy try to . . .

Dee It's okay Mack.

Toilane (*pointing to Mercy*) You know! You know, cause you heard her tell me that it was mine. You were here. Tell them, tell them what ya heard.

Dee My sister would be only too happy to tell you what she heard, we have nothing to hide.

Mercy Would you excuse me please?

She leaves.

Pegs I don't know what that says to the rest of youse, but I sure as hell know what it says to me.

Mack Dee, what's happening?

54

Dee Oh for God's sake, it's just Merc, she's a flake, you know Merc, she's . . . a flake.

Mack Dee, I don't understand, what's . . .

Toilane I understand. I understand. I understand that I been used. I been used in her sick fantasies and I been – (*near hysteria, makes terrible noise*) You loved me. You loved me. You said that you loved me. You said you loved me and you asked me to – you said that you were hornier than you'd ever been, that you were wetter for me than . . .

Dee slaps him.

You fuck ya fuckin cunt whore fuck. You're giving my baby away. Because you don't want it and I'm not good enough, you throw me away like garbage and now my baby, now my baby my . . .

Toilane has been holding Dee by the arm. He throws her off at the end of his speech. Mack, hearing this, realizing that it is genuine, grabs his coat to go.

Dee Mackie, for god's sake, you don't believe the ravings of this . . .

Mack He's not raving, he's real . . .

Dee No he's not.

Mack I know you Dee, you forget. What game are you playing, eh? What fuckin game?

He runs out.

Dee Maaaaaaaaaaackieeeeee.

She turns around and knocks over her easel and a chair.

Get out of my house. Or I'll light you on fire I'll light you on fire, get out of my house.

Pegs (*grabs her*) listen to me. You *think* what is right,

55

I just want you to stop all this bull roar and *think* what is right. Can you do that?

Dee Get out.

Pegs We're going. We just wanted to drop by to inform ya that we will have our child. Whatever we have to do, wherever we have to go, we will have our child. Come on, son. And don't try and run away cause we'll find ya. You better believe we will.

They go.

SCENE TWENTY-ONE

Mercy It's soo lovely outside, the ice on the trees is just you know, it's like the day that Mummy died, we'd been in that dark hospital room all day, holding her head trying to help her breathe, and then the breath gettin lighter and lighter until I thought we'd all stop breathing . . . we'd all . . . rise. And then it stopped. I opened the door to the hall and a group of doctors were in a huddle and they suddenly laughed, roared like a big audience and I told them to shut up, my mother had just died, and then I walked down the back stairs and stepped out the door and the snow shone white, and these huge icy trees just . . . showing . . . themselves . . . showing. And I was so startled . . . to hear my own breath . . . keep . . . on . . .

Pause.

I found this in your drawer. The locket, little silver heart, that Daddy gave you for your special club. 'Ich bin dein' . . . what does that mean?

*Raymond is looking through a book of medieval
German poetry and he finds and reads the following
poem, translating himself.*

Raymond
Du bist mein
Ich bin dein
Des sollst du gewiss sein
Du bist verschlossen
In meinem Herzen
Verloren ist das Schlusselein
Du musst immer drinnen sein.

*Now, with understanding of the significance of the
poem.*

. . . You are locked in my heart
The key is lost
You will always have to stay inside it . . .
For always.

Act Two

Toilane's place, very clean now. Mum has moved in temporarily. She comes in and lies down on the floor right away with her feet up.

Toilane *(after waiting for her to speak)* Well?

Pegs This back is gonna be the death of me.

Toilane What'd he say?

Pegs I got my arthritis puffin up my wrists. My stomach turnin into Mount St Helens every five minutes. I don't know how I keep on keepin on.

Toilane Mum, what'd he say?

Pegs Blood tests. It all hinges on blood tests.

Toilane Blood tests?

Pegs And even that can't tell us for sure.

Toilane But we know. I know it's mine, she told me.

Pegs Don't stand up in a court of law.

Toilane Why not?

Pegs It's her word against yours. She charge you with assault, who they gonna believe?

Toilane Her?

Pegs Yes her. Not only will they believe her but they could send you to jail for her. They could, unless we fight with everything we got. I'm serious Toi, this is no laughing matter.

Toilane Oh. Fuck. Shit.

Pegs That's right.

Toilane Jail?

Pegs That's what I said.

Toilane Jail. Fuck. I'm not doin time again, I . . . fuck.
Fuck. Mum, maybe we should, like, maybe we should
just like, forget it . . . eh? I'm not goin down the river no
way, I'm not going down the river again.

Pegs *Is that your baby?*

Toilane Yes.

Pegs Are you gonna fight for it?

Toilane I don't know.

Pegs Your dad was a quitter, that's how come he spent
sixteen years in jail, are you a quitter too?

Toilane No.

Pegs All evidence to the contrary, are you a quitter?

Toilane No.

Pegs Are you gonna let the high classes chew ya up
and spit ya out? Are you gonna let them take your baby?
My God I got to hate that class of people, cleanin houses.
I got to near throw up when I seen them comin; they used
to talk to me like ya talk to a dog or a baby; 'Hello, Mrs
Creese, how *are* you today?' This one, Mrs Morrin, I
walk in, we're standin on her kitchen floor, so clean you
could eat off it, and she says to me, she says: 'I don't
know what was wrong with that last cleaning woman but
she just couldn't get this floor clean.' and I'm thinkin '*get
me outa here*.' One day I'm talkin to her and she up and
corrects my grammar. Well I turn around and says 'You

59

think I don't know the correct grammar? I know it's "don't have any" but I say "don't got none." I *choose* "don't got none." I *choose* my grammar, cause I'd rather be dead; I'd rather be dead than be anything like you.' They have us believin we can't talk, we can't dress, and now they have you believin you don't have a right to your child. If you don't fight for your child you're worth even less than they think. Are you listening to me? Are you listening to me? Christ, they've got ya, don't they? They got ya so you don't care about your own blood. Do ya?

Toilane Yes.

Pegs Do ya?

Toilane Yes.

Pegs Well tell 'em.

Toilane I will.

Pegs Tell 'em.

Toilane I – will – declare – war.

Pegs Yeah.

Toilane I will . . . I will . . . I will de . . . clare . . . warrrr.

The siren starts up now, the same siren that sounded when Dee was screaming earlier.

I . . . de . . . clare . . . warrrr!
I . . . de . . . clare . . . warrrr!
I . . . de . . . clare . . . warrrr!

SCENE TWENTY-FOUR

Mercy and Dee walking hand in hand, singing their childhood song.

Mercy *and* **Dee**
We are walking together, in the niice weatherrr
Ohhh what a lovelyyy daaaayy.
We are walking together, in the niice weatherrr –

They laugh because they went off-key.

Dee Now you're not going to falter on the witness stand or walk away like that time at dinner?

Mercy No, I promised you, I promise.

Dee You swear on Mummy's grave?

Mercy Yes, I swear on Mummy's grave.

Dee Oh thank you. You are a good sister.

Mercy Deirdre, do you love me?

Dee nods.

Say 'I love you Mercy' – say it.

Dee (*pause*) I love you Mercy.

Mercy More than anything on this earth?

Dee puts locket around Mercy's neck.

SCENE TWENTY-FIVE

Toilane and Pegs on their way to court. Dressed up. Toilane stops at a water fountain, and drinks.

Pegs What the hell do you think you're doin?

Toilane Having a drink of water, what do you think I'm doing?

Pegs Listen to me, have you ever seen a Chinese have a drink of cold water?

Toilane Well . . . no, I mean, I don't know.

Pegs Well you never have because they never would because they're smart and because they're smart they live to a hundred and five more often than not. Myrtle Chow told me never *ever* to drink a drink of cold water no matter how thirsty you are. Blood goes straight to your stomach to warm ya up and it's game over for your brain. Come to think of it, maybe that's why you're as dumb as you are. Come on, we don't want to be late for court for God's sake.

Toilane I'm not dumb.

Pegs (*swings around*) Did you rape her? Did you try to rape her like she says you done?

Toilane Noooooo. I told ya no no no no no no no no.

Pegs For Christ's sake, you'll get the cops on us. Toilane camm down, camm down, I said camm down okay. It's not that I didn't believe you, it's just that when it comes to young boys and sex, there's somethin so big and dark that even a Mum don't know it so I *just had* to ask you by surprise, that's what the cops do . . . always ask the accused by surprise, it always reveals the truth. And you said no. So I believe you. I believe you alright. Let's just hope to high heaven they do. Gosh darn all those bloody B and E's and auto thefts on your record from when we was living in Burlington. I knew you was goin with a bad crowd but I just wasn't sure how bad. Damn that Kevin Blanchard, *damn* him.

Toilane It's not his fault. Jeez Mum, Kevin's got nothin to do with . . .

Pegs Your past, my son, has everything, but everything to do with your present. Every step of the way counts. They don't miss a trick. Boy, she thinks she got us over a barrel, eh? Lying bitch. Her own sister won't even back her up. She don't have a hope in hell today.

Mack addresses the audience.

Mack When I first saw a girl naked I went into shock. I started shaking, the other kids laughed but I was scared, I was scared. I mean . . . I knew girls were different but I never imagined . . .

Pause.

. . . there used to be these school dances, and we'd go, a bunch of us, and of course the really pretty girls were all taken, and if there were any pretty girls left against the wall, you wouldn't dare ask them, I mean you wouldn't dare because if she turns you down you have to pass her in the halls every day for the rest of the year. *No way.* So I used to ask this one . . . I didn't even know her name but she'd always be there, with her friend, all covered in makeup, fat with a short skirt, big barrette in her hair to look prettier, and one time me and the guys had just been walking around all night, going to the washroom for a smoke, you know, the usual shit, and I was gettin sick of it, I wanted, you know, to touch a girl, so this slow dance came up and I tapped her on the shoulder. I didn't even say anything. She looked at me . . . she had nice eyes . . . and she came onto the dance floor, I held her so close, so close I swear I could have crushed her, so of course you know, I got an erection and it would be, well, up against her, she would just bury her head in my shoulder and we'd stay in this clutch . . . we barely moved . . . for the whole song. Then at the end of the song, I'd just turn around and

walk away without looking at her. I never said hello to
her in the halls. When my buddies asked me why I was
dancing with that 'pig' I said she let me dry hump her
on the dance floor. If I'm being punished, somehow, for
that, now, I guess I deserve it. I guess I do.

SCENE TWENTY-SEVEN

*Court corridor. Pegs comes out after having talked to the
lawyer.*

Pegs Toi? Honey? . . . we have to drop . . . the suit.

Toilane What?

Pegs The lawyer believes, is *sure*, that with that sister
backin her up now those girls will send you up for twenty
years. Jail killed your father; it would most certainly kill
you. I don't want to lose the both of youse.

Toilane But . . . I thought you said –

Pegs It doesn't matter what I said . . . honey, they've
brought us to our knees.

Mercy passes. Pegs grabs her.

Hey –

Mercy Please let me go.

Pegs We're human beings. We're not animals you know.

Mercy I didn't say you were an animal.

Pegs Why are you so afraid of her?

Mercy Because . . . I love her.

She wriggles free, runs away.

*Toilane is on the same ramp that he began the play with,
apologizing to the judge so that he won't be charged
with malicious prosecution. In court, Toilane on stand.*

Toilane And I . . . apol – apulol-o-app – I m sorry . . .
for makin up lies to the court . . . I'm . . . real real real
sorry and I'll never do it . . . again . . . (*whispers*) I'll
never do it again.

*Same day, after winning in court, Dee and Mercy are in
a victory dance. On the canvas is a grotesque painting of
a nine-month-old foetus.*

Mercy Whooooo. Whooo hoooooo. Oh God.

She flops down on the couch.

We won.

Dee Yes.

Pause.

We did the right thing didn't we? Don't you think?

Mercy (*takes off shoes*) I'm just glad they don't live here
any more.

She prepares tea.

Dee He couldn't have handled a child, I mean there's
no way.

Mercy . . . Do you want some tea?

Dee Merc? Don't you think?

65

Mercy goes out to make the tea.

Uh.

Mercy What's that, a kick?

Dee *Big* kick in the ribs. Hey, little one? You getting restless? You want out, to the Johnsons? Hey Merc, don't you *love* the Johnsons?

Mercy They seem nice.

Dee They're *fabulous*, fabulous people, Merc, the kid will thank me on its *knees* in twenty years. For sure. Oogh.

Mercy What's wrong, did something happen?

Dee (*checking under her skirt*) No no it's just . . . a leak, I think a trickle – amniotic fluid, a . . . oh, there's the mucous plug . . . (*wraps it in kleenex*)

Mercy Does that mean . . .

Dee No, no, I told you, it's just a leak, a trickle of water, it means there's a tear in one of the sacs, that's all, a little tear . . . it could have torn it with its . . . fingernail.

Mercy Are you sure we shouldn't go to hospital?

Dee No, I'm fine, I'd just like that tea I think.

Mercy Sure, sure, (*brings it*) here. Do you want something to eat?

Dee almost swoons.

Dee? Are you alright?

Dee Ohh. Nooo. Ohhh. Oh my God, oh my God, a lion a lion, I can . . . see – a – a – lion, a lion, breaking through the wall a lion roaring, all the stones breaking, flying, roaring. Stop.

Mercy What do you mean, you see this in your mind?

Dee A lion. . . . stop it. stop it.

Mercy Let's go to hospital, Dee, come on.

Dee Aaaaahh!

Mercy Let's go to hospital.

Dee No, no, no it's just lack of sleep . . . it's lack of sleep, it's lack of sleep.

Mercy I know, I'll make you some hot milk, that'll make you feel better, let me make you some hot milk.

Dee It's lack of sleep.

She lies down on the couch, shudders. Knock at the door. Mercy gets the door.

Pegs We just . . . my son just wanted to make an apology to youse, he feels bad for what he done, and . . .

Mercy Oh there's no need for that.

Pegs Oh, yes there is. We caused you people a lot of trouble and expense, and we want to apologize. Do you mind . . .

Mercy Well . . .

Dee No, Merc, I'm going to bed, I . . . Really, there's no need for an apology, I . . .

Pegs Oh certainly there is, we'll just sit down and have a cup of tea with ya . . . and ya see we want to be friends, we want to put all this mess behind us, and you know what I mean?

Dee It's just that I was about to go to bed, and . . .

Pegs For God's sake give us this, girl, you had us evicted you made my son lie in court, for God's sake, let us be your friends. For his sake, not for mine, believe me if it was up to me . . .

67

Dee Okay, I'm sorry, please, have a seat. Mercy? Would you like to give these people some tea?

Mercy Okay. What do you take?

Toilane No milk, two sugar please.

Pegs Just clear for me, thanks.

Mercy One clear, one double clear.

Dee So . . . how do you like your new place?

Pegs Oh we like it fine. We'd been wanting to get outa here anyway, so really, you done us a favour.

Dee It wasn't anything to do with me whatever you may think, really, I hardly know the landlord.

Pegs Oh that's okay.

Dee Really.

Pegs I believe ya. That's a nice picture.

Dee Thank you, a friend did it.

Pegs Oh? What's it supposed to be?

Dee It's uh . . . whatever you like . . .

Pegs Oh I get it.

Mercy Some biscuits?

Pegs Oh, not for me, got to watch the old waistline.

Mercy You don't have a weight problem.

Pegs Oh that's very kind but I do. I weighed ninety pounds when I married Toi's father. (*to Dee*) Now you certainly don't have a weight problem . . . how much you gained with the baby?

Dee Oh . . . I don't know, I guess about twenty-five

pounds. I don't really keep track.

Pegs No more than twenty, my doctor said. He said if I gained more than twenty he'd hang me.

Dee (*pause*) Did you?

Pegs Seventy-five pounds and I lived on chicken noodle soup. I'm serious.

As Pegs talks, Dee starts to go into mild labour.
Of course, we have to speed things up: every half
minute or so.

Mercy Here's the tea . . . double sugar for you and clear for you.

Pegs Thanks dear. Yes, as I say, he's going into retail management, what's the name of the store Toilane?

Toilane Jones Work Warehouse, it's just like work clothes, sort of, and I'm just at the till, Ma, it's not management.

Pegs But darlin, nobody stays at the till, certainly no son of mine, oh no you're far too smart to stay at the till.

Mercy I worked in retail for a while.

Pegs Did you now dear? Well did you get managerial?

Mercy No, no, I didn't.

Pegs Good tea, what kind is it?

Starts to notice Dee is in pain.

Dee Darjeeling, I think, isn't it Merc?

Pegs That's Indian isn't it?

Dee I'm not sure.

Pegs You okay dear? You look a little uncomfortable.

69

Dee Oh, I'm fine, it's just . . . the baby's foot sticks in my ribs . . . I . . . think I am gonna have to go lie down, actually.

Pegs Little tightness in the chest?

Dee Yuh, I just . . .

Pegs Here, lie down here, here, we'll sit in chairs, Toi can sit on the floor, we'll just finish our tea and we'll go.

Dee Really I –

Pegs There, there, just lie yourself down, I was a RNA I know what I'm talking about, a little company's not gonna kill you.

Dee (*lies down*) Okay, just a few minutes, though.

Pegs Comfy now? You'll be okay. Well. This is like a reunion after so long. Eh? Just a bunch of friends, after all that's happened? Who would thought it . . . Toilane knows he mighta made a mistake . . . I do, however, think it would be a nice gesture if you . . . admit, just for me bein his mum, that my son did not assault you.

Dee Oh listen, if I thought you were going to . . .

Pegs No no no now don't get het up. I just want you to tell me whether or not my son assaulted you.

Dee I withdrew the charge. What does it matter.

Pegs It matters to me, I'm his mother.

Dee He knows the truth.

Pegs I think we all know the truth.

Dee Would you please leave?

Pegs No. I'm enjoying the reunion; and after what you done to us I think we gotta right . . .

Dee reaches for phone

Toi.

Toilane cuts the phone. Dee gets up.

Dee What is this?

Mercy runs to door. Toilane blocks the door.

Pegs We want . . . to be treated . . . hospitable by you. We want the respect . . . we deserve. Now sit down and talk nice.

They sit down nervously. Dee's waters break.

Dee Aghhhhh!

Pegs Your waters.

Mercy Deedee are you okay?

Dee It's nothing, nothing.

Pegs Nothing. My dear, your waters broke.

Mercy I really think we ought to be going. Dee, I'll get your coat.

Pegs You're not going anywhere till we've had our visit. Now sit down.

Mercy You're crazy. You're a crazy lady!

Pegs You try to leave and my son will do whatever he has to do to stop you. So sit down.

Mercy Just . . . a short visit, then, please?

Pegs *I want my reunion.*

Dee contracts, bad labour pain throughout this speech.

Huh, speakin of reunions, I got a story. We had our high school reunion last year and of course I didn't want to go,

I'd got so old, fat, you know, but my girl-friend, Janis, she said, oh come on, we're all old and fat, we'll have a ball, get out the rum and cokes, and the taco chips, play a little bingo, have a blast. So finally I thought, oh alright, so I trudged on over with Janis, and I had a pretty good time, and I was sittin at a table havin a pie and coffee with a few girls when one of 'em says, well she says, 'I've had such a nice time, but I just wish to heaven that Peggy Lane had come,' Lane's my maiden name, 'she's always such a laugh.' Well I musta turned three shades a red, I could hardly speak but I did, like a fool, I turned to her and I said, 'But Marjorie, here I am, I'm Peggy. Didn't you see me?' Well then *she* turned three shades of red and she *said*, 'Well, yes, I did, but I wouldn't have known you . . . your *face*.' My face, had got so . . . it's true I guess, I don't look nothing like my wedding pictures. Toi don't believe me when I tell him how pretty I was.

Toilane Yes I do.

Pegs Isn't that a funny one? You okay, dear? Looks like you're gonna have a baby in a day or so. Toi? I guess we'd better be goin.

Pegs gets up, Toilane is still.

Toi?

Toilane I don't want to go.

Pegs Toi, the lady is going to have a baby, good God –

Toilane I want . . . my baby.

Pegs But Toi, the courts ruled.

Toilane I don't care what the courts ruled. I want my baby.

Pegs Well you can have another one, there are plenty of girls out there.

Toilane I want my baby with the woman I love.

Pegs Toi, you don't love her, you had a silly crush, now –

Toilane I love her and she loves me. I love you. You love me and you are going to have my baby and I . . . want it. I want to take care of it. Mum, you know you said if there was anything I really needed you would be there for me, you'd help me out.

Pegs Toi.

Toilane You said to trust you, you said you'd come through, are you gonna help me?

Pegs Help you what?

Toilane Deliver the baby.

Pegs Toi for God's sake, what if there's complications?

Toilane What?

Pegs If that baby won't come out, she might have to have a Caesarian you know, be cut out.

Toilane Well you done that, you done them things you said, when you worked in the hospital.

Pegs Toi, this is . . . against the law, this is . . .

Dee is about to vomit.

Do you need to throw up dear?

She gets something.

Here, if you want to throw up.

Dee does.

Dee I want to go to hospital, I want . . .

Toilane I want my child. I'm gonna have my child.

Dee You can't do this, this is sick, this is . . .

73

Pegs My son wants his child and he got a right and you know he does. Now nobody's gonna hurt you. We're just gonna take what is rightfully ours.

Dee Just for Christ's sake, can't you just leave. Merceeee!

Mercy stands up. Stands on her tippytoes. Lifts her hands high in the air. Eyes wide, turns around and walks out.

Toilane Hey.

Pegs It's okay, let her go.

Toilane But what if she drops a dime, Ma?

Pegs She won't.

Toilane She won't?

Pegs She won't.

Dee Oh no oh nooo it's coming again it's coming again the big lion is coming down to crush me to crush me oh no oh no ohhh I can't stand it I can't stand it uhhhhhhhh Mackie, Mackie, please, please, take me to hospital, I think I'm gonna die, I really think I'm gonna die.

Pegs That's what they all say dear, the schoolyards are full.

Toilane I'm your husband now. I'll help ya through it.

Dee Oh God, oh God, I must be in hell, that's what it is. I died and I'm in hell, or I know. It's a dream, that's what it is, a terrible nightmare, oh God, oh – aghhhhh! Let me wake up please let me wake up.

Pegs (*to Toilane*) I think it's time we brought her into the bedroom, Toi, she'll be more comfortable there.

Dee Nooooo!

Toilane helps Dee into the bedroom.

(*To Toilane*) You . . . you won't let me die will you? Will you?

Toilane I love you, Dee, I'd never let you die.

Dee, crying, collapses into his arms.

SCENE THIRTY

This could be a dream. Mercy, stunned in courtyard. Raymond walks by. She is just staring.

Raymond (*after looking several times*) Excuse me, excuse me but your name wouldn't happen to be . . . Mercia . . . would it?

Mercy Yes. Who are you?

Raymond Raymond. Raymond Brisson from . . . I used to drive you to school when you were . . . a schoolgirl . . . in Montreal . . . you were about fifteen, I believe – St Francis.

Mercy Raymond.

Raymond Yes, that's right – Raymond . . . How strange to see you here, do you live . . . in one of these apartments?

Mercy Yes. Do you?

Raymond Well I keep a small flat here . . . you see I teach here twice a week, so I go back and forth from the country.

Mercy It's . . . funny to see you, like seeing the house I grew up in with different people living in it, it's funny.

Raymond Yes, it's that way seeing you too. As if – a – light – switched.

75

Mercy Oh Raymond, I love the way you touched me.

Raymond (*blushes deeply*) . . . Are you alright? You seem to be . . .

Mercy What, what do I seem?

Raymond Well, it looks as if you've had a bit of a shock.

Mercy It's just that I see you, and all I want, all I really want is for you to touch me again.

Raymond It's lovely to see you.

Mercy Oh Raymond, I've had so many . . . dreams about you, you know nobody's touched me in the same . . . way, made the honey – pour –

Raymond Say, would you like a cup of tea, why don't you come up to my flat and I'll get you a cup of tea and a – a – biscuit.

Mercy Yeah, I'd like to come up to your flat, I'll come up to your flat and have a nice cup of tea and then I'm going to take off my clothes and I'm going to spread my legs and you're going to . . . make love to me. We never went all the way, you know, in the car, we only ever did everything but.

Raymond (*clearly aroused*) Well, let's just see about that tea first of all and sitting you down . . .

Mercy I dreamed about you all the time.

Raymond and Mercy hold position.

SCENE THIRTY-ONE

Toilane and Pegs and baby on a bus in the night. Toilane goes to light a cigarette.

Pegs No smokin with the baby, Toi, you should know that.

Toilane Oh right. How is she?

Pegs Oh Tracy Meg is just fine, sleepin like a baby.

Toilane Ever cute. You sure you brought enough formula?

Pegs I brought you up didn't I? Trust me for God's sake.

Toilane I do, I do, I'm just . . . nervous, you know. What if they catch up with us?

Pause.

Ma, do you think she's okay?

Pegs Who?

Toilane Deedree.

Pegs Sure she's okay. She never wanted a baby and now she doesn't have one.

Toilane I love her though Mum you know, I still love her.

Pegs Don't be a sap.

Toilane I'll love her till the day I die. Hey. Do you think she looks like me?

Pegs I think she looks like your father, if you want to know the truth.

Toilane But she looks like our side, like, you can definitely see it's mine.

Pegs Oh no question about it, the minute I saw her.

Toilane It's like there's a well, you know, and when I seen her, Tracy? Something pumped that water up and it filled my whole head, you know, it filled my whole head.

Waiting room. Mercy and Mack.

Mercy But I betrayed her, I betrayed my own sister.
I thought, you know, I thought it was the right thing.
I wanted to do the right thing for once in my life. I'm
sorry you know but I'm not at the same time. Do you
know what I mean? I mean I'm sorry but I'm not sorry
I'm not I'm sorry I'm not I'm sorry I'm not I'm not I'm
sorry.

> *They go into the hospital room. Dee is in bed, breasts
> bandaged. She wakes up.*

Dee Mercy.

> *She reaches for her. Mercy goes and hugs Dee.*

Mercy. Where's the baby?

Mercy Dee, she's . . . she's in the nursery. She's in the
nursery with the other babies. She's fine.

Dee A girl? She's a girl?

Mercy Yes, a little girl.

Dee And they didn't get her? Him and his mother, they
didn't get her?

Mercy No Dee, they left. They left and we went to the
hospital and you had the baby. You just had a very
rough time. You had a very rough birth.

Dee Then it was a dream? You mean it was a dream?
But I was so sure it was real, no, it couldn't have been a
dream, you're lying to me, you're lying . . .

Mercy Mackie –

Dee You're lying, where's my baby, where's my . . .

Mack She's here, I told you Dee. She's . . . okay, really.

Dee She is? She is?

Mack The baby is just fine. The nurses are taking care of her in the nursery – she's in the nursery.

Dee But I was sure that it wasn't a dream. Mackie? Mackie?

Mack You're okay Dee, you're gonna be okay.

Dee Are you gonna stay with me? You aren't going to leave?

Mack No, I'm not going to leave.

Dee Cause, cause I want to keep our baby now, Mack, I want to keep her. The Johnsons aren't here, are they, get them away, get them away.

Mack I just think you ought to get some rest now Deirdre.

Dee But I want to see my baby, show me my baby, show me my baby. My God, you're on fire, your eyes are on fire. Your eyes are on fire.

Mack interjects throughout the speech with 'Shh' and 'No, no.'

Mercy, Mercy, your face your face is burning, burning, burning, white. I want to talk to my mother. I want to talk to my mother.

Mercy But Dee, Mummy's dead, she's dead.

Mack *Dee.*

Dee I know, I know she's dead, I know she's dead but I want to talk to her, I want to . . . talk to her, I want . . .

to tell her that I'm . . . sorry. I want to say I'm sorry.
I'm sorrry. I'm sorrrry. I'm sorrrry.

SCENE THIRTY-THREE

*Raymond speaking to Mercy, but it doesn't matter if she
is on stage or not. He should not be speaking directly
to her.*

Raymond I dreamed about you too, you know, several
times a year every time the season changed. Swimming,
swimming in cold blue water, clear; striped fish and
dark, inky seals jumping around us, and I turn, and look
at you and your eyes, your eyes are toooo . . . blue . . .
And then I'd wake up, look out the window and see the
first snowfall, or the leaves had turned . . . overnight . . .

SCENE THIRTY-FOUR

Pegs and Toilane in hotel room. Light flashing outside.

Toilane Sudbury on a Saturday night eh?

Pegs Sssshh shhh. I think she's down.

Toilane (*sits down*) Mum.

Pegs Yuh.

Toilane I wanted to tell you . . . that . . . like . . . I
wanted to apologize.

Pegs What for?

Toilane For that time . . . when I was in grade four that
time, and . . . we were having the goodbye thing . . .
party or something for Mrs Lamb.

Pegs She was your favourite teacher.

Toilane And you came to get me just when I's gonna give my present to her, I was just giving it to her and there you were and I was so embarrassed you looked so . . . bright or something, too bright or too big . . . so . . . I said for you to get out. I said, 'Get out of here mother,' and you did, you ran, crying down the hill, and broke your high heel. I felt so bad about that high heel, about you breakin it on that hill cause of me. Okay.

Pegs It was damn stupid of me, I knew how much that teacher meant to you, I shouldn't have come.

Toilane Mum, how come she breathes so fast?

Pegs Babies do, they breathe fast . . . look at her little face, will ya?

Toilane Mum? What . . . do you think she's dreamin? Do you think she's dreamin?

Pegs I don't know. Little rose.

Toilane Little rose.

Pegs Ohhhh. Boy. I'm gonna have to sit down, I'm not feelin too good.

Toilane What's the matter?

Pegs should not be sitting on the bed, but on a chair beside the bed.

Pegs I think it was that sandwich, the Toasted Western, I think it musta been bad.

Toilane Yah? What . . . is it your stomach or –

Pegs No, my head, it feels like my head's on fire, like white . . .

*Dee opens a door. A light blinds the audience. She walks
forward on the ramp towards the audience. The audience,
to her, is the nursery. She is looking for her baby. She
feels purified – through birth – and also through understanding her self-hatred, her guilt about her mother –
she is now able to love after having grappled with her
'shadow' or 'animal'. She is infused with this love. She
sees the baby somewhere in the audience (not picking
out an individual, of course).*

Dee Ohhhh. Which . . . one are you, baby? Which . . .
Oh. I see you. I see you now. Oh. You are so . . .
beautiful. Yes. Yes. I want you baby, I want you forever
because I . . . love you. I *love* you. Oh. Oh. Your eyes
are opening . . . Hello. Hello. Hello. Hello.

SCENE THIRTY-SIX

*We cross-fade to Toilane. In the hotel room, hotel light
still flashing. Pegs passed out or maybe dead in chair.
Toilane stands there, holding the baby, bewildered.*

Toilane Mum?